'You let me 「 time you be man!'

'I didn't ask you here to rake up the past, Mel. You help companies that are in trouble, and, loath as I am to admit it, I need your advice. They say you're the best.'

'I don't come cheap, Jade.'

'You never did.'

'But *you* did, didn't you? Bargain basement.'

The insult was unbearable. 'Your sole purpose for being here is to humiliate me for what you think I did to you four years ago, isn't it?'

'I came here to lay a few ghosts before I make the big commitment.'

Jade stared at him, her dark eyes wide with pain. 'Y-you're going to...to be married?'

Natalie Fox was born and brought up in London and has a daughter, two sons and two grandchildren. Her husband, Ian, is a retired advertising executive, and they now live in a tiny Welsh village. Natalie is passionate about her cats—two strays brought back from Spain where she lived for five years—and equally passionate about gardening and writing romance. Natalie says she took up writing because she absolutely *hates* going out to work!

MAN TROUBLE!

BY
NATALIE FOX

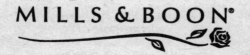

MILLS & BOON®

All the characters in this book have no existence outside the imagination of the author, and have no relation whatsoever to anyone bearing the same name or names. They are not even distantly inspired by any individual known or unknown to the author, and all the incidents are pure invention.

First published in Great Britain 1997
Harlequin Mills & Boon Limited,
Eton House, 18-24 Paradise Road, Richmond, Surrey TW9 1SR

© Natalie Fox 1997

ISBN 0 263 80030 X

Set in Times Roman 10 on 11½ pt.
01-9703-59040 C1

Printed and bound in Great Britain
by Mackays of Chatham PLC, Chatham

CHAPTER ONE

'MEL BIAGGIO for you, Jade,' came over the intercom.

Jade Ritchie took a nervous breath. Well, this was it, what she had been waiting for all week. He was here, and the fact that he had agreed to see her at all was something, she supposed. She cleared her throat to respond to her secretary, striving to sound cool and efficient because she knew Mel would be able to hear her voice as he waited by the reception desk and the last thing she wanted him to know was that she was terrified of facing him again.

'Send him in, Diane, and hold all my calls till he's gone.'

Jade's index finger stayed suspended over the buzzer, as if by depressing the button again she could wish all this away. But it was impossible. Her company needed a troubleshooter and, as Nicholas had sagely advised, when you were in trouble you didn't mess with second best. There were other troubleshooters, of course, but unfortunately none with Mel's track record of unparalleled success. He had the Midas touch when it came to rescuing companies from the brink of bankruptcy. And Jade's company needed rescuing and, miserably, the best happened to be Mel Biaggio, the Mel of her painful past.

Jade felt sick inside and bravely stood up ready to face him. She was of medium height but her small bone structure put her in the class of petite. His pocket-sized princess, he'd used to call her, and her bones had always melted when he'd murmured the endearment in her ear.

Now, after four years without sight of him, she wondered whether if he spoke those tender words again those same silly bones would melt. She shivered at the thought, flicked her jet hair away from her neck and fixed her dark eyes on the back of the door.

The door opened and instinctively Jade clenched her fists with tension, her polished nails digging into her palms, but the pain was nothing compared to what was searing her heart. He hadn't changed a bit and she was overwhelmingly disappointed. She had prayed that he'd look different so that she could look at him and wonder what she had ever seen in him in the first place. But life wasn't that obliging.

Folding down the collar of his navy cashmere coat, he approached. He was still as wretchedly good-looking as ever, his hair as black as ever, not even a wisp of silver to soften the dark severity of it. Tiny lines around his dark grey eyes were the only sign that an eternity had passed since they had last met.

She understood why gossip columnists took such interest in him. When she had known him he hadn't yet hit the tabloid columns but he had since made up for lost ground. Classed as one of the most eligible bachelors in the financial City, he had certainly earned his title. He'd had more on-off relationships than a lighthouse. With punishing, morbid curiosity Jade had brooded over those reports, hardly able to believe them at times, because surely that wasn't the Mel she had known and loved? So hadn't she had a narrow escape, hadn't time drawn out his true character and wasn't she the lucky one in escaping?

As he came to a stop in front of her desk, silent, predatory, cold, her emotions swam with a dizzying effect that totally confused her. She wanted to despise him for the injustice he had done her four years ago, for the

women in his life since, and even for not having had the
decency to age since she had seen him last. But those
silly bones were softening already.

'Mel Biaggio,' Jade breathed levelly, surprising herself
with the evenness of her tone. Her insides were heaving
like an oarless boat on the perimeters of a whirlpool but
at least her voice hadn't failed her.

Not a smile of greeting or even recognition softened
his dark features and Jade's heart floundered helplessly.
A business associate of Nicholas's had arranged this
meeting for her, someone Mel had helped in the past.
Nicholas didn't know Mel personally and yet he was the
one inadvertently responsible for the break-up of their
love affair. Jade hadn't enlightened him when Nicholas
had suggested Mel for the job. It was done, over with,
and nothing to do with the present. And yet now Mel
was looking at her as if she were a stranger and the name
Jade Ritchie hadn't registered with him when this meeting
had been set up.

'Jade Ritchie,' he said coldly and unemotionally. 'You
trade under your maiden name—an affectation that
doesn't surprise me.'

Her heart faltered. Of course her name had registered, of course he recognised her. She was mad to think
for a minute that he wouldn't remember their past. How
awful this was, facing him like this. How bitter and harsh
he sounded. He had assumed she'd gone through with
the marriage and the thought sickened her and filled her
with shame.

He'd never believed how much she had loved him,
and how futile her pleas must have sounded that awful
night of her party. But how wrong he had been in not
giving her a chance to explain. She couldn't take all the
blame. He should have listened, and judging by his attitude now it was obvious he hadn't relented. He was

here, facing her, but had she really imagined they could keep this on a business footing after the pain of their past?

'What's in a name, Mel?' she said lightly, almost dismissively. What was the point in enlightening him and saying that she was still single? It wouldn't make any difference to a business arrangement, which was what this meeting was all about, she reminded herself. She forced a thin smile. 'Business is business. Won't you sit down?'

'Is it going to be worth my while?' The question came out wrapped in a tone of cynicism, with a small, derisive smile to accompany it.

It's hopeless, Jade thought miserably. There's too much pain and not enough cool control. And yet she willed it from deep inside her because four years in the ad agency business had taught her that when the going got tough the tough got going. She had swallowed her pride and was standing here now, facing the man she had once thought she was going to spend the rest of her life with, because she wasn't a wimp and she was going to fight to keep her company afloat, whatever the personal cost!

'That's for you to decide, not me,' she returned coolly. She sat down and he followed suit, sweeping aside his coat and lowering himself into the seat across the desk from her. His keeping his coat on seemed ominous to Jade. He didn't look as if he was going to afford her any decent amount of time to discuss her problem. Was he simply here out of curiosity, to see what a mess she had made of her life without him at her side?

'Mel...' she started again, levelling her dark eyes at him, striving for a businesslike tone to cover her obvious awareness of him. He seemed to fill the office, all man, all power, seeming to draw the very air from the room.

She swallowed hard. 'This is all very difficult for me. I would have sold my soul to the devil and my body to the highest bidder if I'd thought by doing so I could avoid calling you in, but—' she gave a small, hopeless shrug of her narrow shoulders '—I need your help.'

She watched his eyes for some kind of softening but almost instantly knew it was hopeless. He was unflinching in his cold scrutiny of her. Wasn't he aware of the enormous effort of will and swallowing of pride that had gone into her decision to call him in?

He held her gaze, eyes hard and implacable, and then suddenly those eyes blazed across the front of her open jacket, taking in the rise of her breasts against her cream silk shirt under the crisp designer tailoring.

Jade tensed, inwardly shocked that even a blatantly sexual glance like that could upset her so. It brought their past flooding back to her—the depth of passion so easily aroused by a mere glance at each other, the love, the lust, the need for each other.

It was as if he knew what she was aware of: the charge between them. He tutted mockingly. 'I wouldn't put much of a price on your soul, darling, but that body of yours, if my memory serves me well, would bring a packet if marketed more sensually than in that austere outfit you are wearing.'

The words shocked Jade so deeply that she was rendered speechless for an embarrassing moment. She felt the heat of humiliation rise up her throat, but fought to control it and succeeded. She'd been wrong to think he hadn't changed. Maybe he hadn't physically, but his cruelty had never been so apparent before. But perhaps he had always been like this and she just hadn't seen it, love being blind. She wouldn't allow him to get to her now, though, not after this length of time. She didn't have to take this.

Slowly she got to her feet. This meeting had served one purpose if nothing else—shown her that she'd wasted four years of torn emotions on this man.

'I'm sorry I troubled you, Mel,' she said quietly. 'Just one thing before you leave,' she added pointedly. He would go, of course, because he had never come here with the intention of helping anyway. 'Why did you come here armed with humiliation and insults when you dished them out so effectively four years ago?'

He took his time getting to his feet, lazily rearranging his cashmere overcoat over his superbly cut navy blue suit before answering her, the languorous movement stage-managed to grate on her nerves, she felt sure. Even his low tone was gauged for effect.

'When it came to trading humiliation, Jade, you beat me hands down. Whatever I said to you could never match what you put me through that horrendous night.'

He put his palms down on her desk and leaned closer to her, eyes dark and menacing. He was so close she could smell the seductive cologne that came from the heat of his body. A scent so evocative that she had to clench her fists to stop herself swaying into it and losing her cool control.

'Did you really believe I would come here with an open heart and a willingness to haul your company out of the bankruptcy pit?' he went on scathingly, his eyes darkening even more savagely. 'You have some nerve, Jade. Four years ago you indulged in an affair with me while you were committed to another man. You let me love you, we made love, and all the time you belonged to another man. I've often wondered just how far you would have gone with the charade if your father hadn't made that engagement announcement at your twenty-first birthday party...'

'Mel,' Jade cried, 'please don't!' Oh, she couldn't bear it. She bit her lip in anguish, drawing on her reserves of cool. She might have known he would never forget it; she might have known he'd seen his chance for revenge and that was why he was here.

'Please don't?' he echoed harshly. 'You even talk the way you used to. You used me four years ago, Jade, and the only explanation I could ever come up with was that you were such a rich, spoilt child you wanted to possess everything you set your eyes on, including me.'

Jade's cool shattered like thin ice. The injustice of his words hurt so deeply that she felt physically winded. He was wrong, so very wrong to believe that of her.

'It was never like that, Mel,' she breathed painfully. 'I might have had an over-privileged childhood because my father was making up for the absence of a mother, but that wasn't my fault, and he was only doing what he thought best in his usual bulldozing way. I wasn't spoilt, never that. I didn't want to possess you in that way, like a trophy. I loved you—'

'You don't know the meaning of the word love,' he snapped back. 'When you love someone you don't two-time them—'

'I didn't two-time anyone, Mel,' Jade insisted, though she knew she was wasting her breath. 'I know how it must have looked but you didn't even give me the chance—'

'To explain?' he exploded. 'What needed explaining? Your father said it all in his announcement speech. His wonderful daughter was that night betrothed to his greatest friend's son, Nicholas Fields. My God, Jade, what was going on in that beautiful head of yours that night? You insisted I came to the party to humiliate me and—'

'Stop it!' she cried at last, her fingers going to her temples with the anguish of his agonising reminders. She had relived that terrible moment so many times and it never got any better, only worse. Humiliation had been the order of the night. None had escaped from it. Not Mel, Nicholas nor herself.

The only one immune to the whole horrible experience had been her father. Her powerful, manipulative father who ploughed through life not considering anyone's feelings but his own. His ill-timed engagement announcement had stemmed from his own wish to bond the two families together. She and Nicholas had practically grown up together and, though very close, hadn't dreamt of marriage... But they might have *drifted* into it if Mel hadn't stepped into her life and shown her what real love was all about. Though there had never been any formal commitment to Nicholas it had always been accepted between the two families that they were a couple. But that hadn't been a consideration when Mel had asked her out. She hadn't felt as if she *belonged* to Nicholas.

Mel had been so different—a high-flyer and a very powerful man. He had swept her off her feet. Half-Italian, he was magnetically attractive, in looks and charisma and everything else. In no time at all she had known she was in love with him, and he had loved her too. And then, at her party, it had all gone horribly wrong.

But though she blamed her father she knew deep in her heart that she had made a grave mistake in not mentioning the existence of Nicholas to Mel before that night. But would it have made any difference? Somehow she doubted it because she hadn't taken into account Mel's fiery Italian ancestry. *Any* man, friend or otherwise, in competition with Mel Biaggio wasn't on.

'I didn't ask you here to rake up the past, Mel,' she told him in a resigned tone. 'It was all useless then and is equally useless now.'

She took a deep breath and met his dark gaze bravely. Having to plead with him for help was worse than anything she'd had to do in her life before. She *did* have to take this—his spiteful recriminations for a lost love; she had no choice. These last few weeks had driven all pride from her. She had employees to consider, people who had worked for her father before her, new young talent she'd given a chance to in difficult economic times. She owed them and she owed her father for having had enough confidence in her to hand over control of the company and take off for a new life in the South of France.

'I want us to forget we have a past, Mel. You help companies that are in trouble,' she went on, trying not to humble herself too much in case he leapt on it and hurt her more. This was hard enough. 'And, loath as I am to admit it, I'm in trouble. I need your help and your advice, Mel, on a professional basis. It's your job. It's what you do. And... and they say you're the best.'

'And you reckon you deserve the best, do you?'

Jade tilted her chin, biting back the pain caused by his sarcasm. 'My staff and the company deserve the best and that is why I wanted you. It's obvious flattery isn't going to get me anywhere with you but that doesn't alter the fact that you are the best. I want your help in pinpointing where I've gone wrong—'

'You never were very sharp at pinpointing right from wrong,' he said wearily.

Jade shut her eyes briefly in sufferance and when she focused on him again she knew she had to swallow all his insults and persist.

'Yes, I've made mistakes in my life and my work and I'm not afraid to admit to them. I've shelved my pride too, which is something you might be interested in learning from. If I can handle the past I'm sure you can.' She took a long breath. 'Mel, I need your expertise. I need your advice. This is a business arrangement, nothing else. I have the problem and you have the solution. Won't you even consider it?'

Her plea hung in the air with nowhere to go, because Mel looked as if he wasn't about to give it a home. He looked as if he didn't care a damn about anything or anyone in the world, especially not her and her predicament. He was still gazing at her with contempt, making her feel inadequate and at fault, and she suffered it all because her back was against the wall.

'What's the problem?' he asked quietly.

Jade controlled the leap of her heart. He still stood stiffly in front of her, not making any move to sit down again and discuss it with her. She wondered if she should buzz for coffee; it might relax him, persuade him to take a seat, and make her feel more at ease. Perhaps it would be too presumptuous. He'd only asked what the problem was; that wasn't an acceptance that he would help her.

'I'm hoping you can tell me,' she told him, handing him a weighty file she had prepared earlier, detailing their current financial status, projects—existing and proposed, staffing—everything that was relevant. 'It's been a bad year—not disastrous, but another year like this and it could be. I'm loath to involve my father and I decided to ask your advice and . . .' She stopped, realising he probably didn't know her father had handed the running of the company over to her.

'Four years ago . . . just after . . . just after I turned twenty-one . . . my father allowed me to take over the agency.' It had been her lifeline at the time. Just what she had needed to help her get over Mel. 'You may remember I came here from art school and a year's business course in America ... Anyway, Daddy had had enough of London Life and wanted out. He still owns the company but I run it and make all the decisions. He lives in the South of France now. He has a new love in his life and ...'

Jade swallowed hard. Mel was flicking through the file, evidently not in the least bit interested in her private life or that of her father.

She went on, 'Everything was going fine with the agency till last year when my top graphic artist left ...' He wasn't listening. He didn't care. He wouldn't help. 'He set up on his own and took with him a lot of the company's clients ... some of the best clients ... and the best advertising.'

Mel looked up then, eyes as steely and implacable as ever. 'You let him?' he said, aghast that she should have allowed such a thing to happen.

Jade bristled at that. 'I didn't know, not till it was too late!' she protested quickly.

'You should always tie up your top staff in contracts they can't get out of. For your own protection,' he told her sternly.

'This is a small agency; I like to think of it as a family business ...'

He shot her a look of pure derision. 'With you as the mother hen, I suppose, all clucking—'

'That's enough, Mel,' Jade interrupted. 'I trust my staff and I'm not ruthless enough to tie them all to contracts,' she argued, though fully understanding his way of thinking. If she'd had the employee in question under a more restrictive contract she wouldn't have lost valuable clients and wouldn't be struggling so hard now as a consequence.

'Trouble is, these days being ruthless pays, Jade,' he told her tightly, his eyes darkening even further as he narrowed them at her. 'Surely your *ruthless* stockbroker husband has taught you something since you were married?'

Her full lips parted in protest. Mel really believed she had gone through with the marriage to Nicholas—and how did he know he was a stockbroker? Had her father mentioned it in his engagement announcement? Had that business associate of Nicholas's, who had arranged all this, named his source?

Jade had sworn Nicholas to secrecy, terrified that her staff would find out that all wasn't well with the company. Whatever, whoever, however, she couldn't let it go. If this was a one-off meeting she could let him go on thinking she was married, but if he took on this assignment he would find out that she wasn't and despise her even more for, as he would see it, yet another deception.

'I...I didn't marry Nicholas,' she told him in a half-whisper she barely heard herself. How could she even consider marriage to *anyone* after the great love they had shared? And how enormously hurtful that he still thought so little of her.

But she hadn't the courage to add that Nicholas was still very much a part of her life. He couldn't help but be, since he shared her London flat with her when he was in town, albeit to save money for when he and his fiancée, Trisha, married and bought their own property. No, her arrangement with Nicholas had no bearing on all this, was nothing to do with Mel. She'd told him the truth—that she hadn't married Nicholas. It was enough.

There was nothing, no reaction whatsoever to her revelation in his gleaming grey eyes. It meant nothing to him and she felt a small sorrow deep in her heart. Hope; she had always lived with it, though she often thought it a silly little hope to hang onto. She even despised herself for the irrationality of it, but deep, deep down inside her she had nurtured the hope that one day he would come back into her life and . . . and care.

'Well, it's a pity you didn't,' he said frostily. 'His business sense might have saved you from this.' He waved the file in his hand and then transferred his attention to its contents again.

At least he hadn't insulted Nicholas by presuming he had no business sense. She waited, shifting her weight from one high heel to the other as he flicked through the pages, reading only what interested him. But was *anything* interesting him? she wondered. His expression didn't change. Finally he tossed the file down on the desk in front of her.

'By the look of those financial statements you can't afford my fees anyway. I don't come cheap, Jade.'

She hardened her heart and stiffened her back. She shouldn't have asked him. She shouldn't have allowed herself to be persuaded by Nicholas that this was the best course of action to take. She should have known it would be hopeless, that Mel wouldn't help her—even if she could afford his wretched fees.

'You never did come cheap, Mel,' she said coldly, and astonishingly this brought a small, thin smile to his lips.

'No, I didn't,' he drawled smoothly. 'But *you* did, didn't you? Bargain basement.'

The insult was unbearable. So painful, she felt almost sick. It was worse than all his other insults that night of her birthday. He had accused her of every moral mis-demeanour in the book of proprieties. She had tried to explain the situation with Nicholas but, up against a barrage of raw accusations and offensive remarks, what chance had she stood? According to proud Mel Biaggio, she had deceived him, hurt him, cheated him and in-sulted him. He never wanted to see her again as long as he lived. It had turned out to be the worst night of her life instead of what should have been one of the happiest.

She watched him come round the side of her desk, her eyes misted by that insult, her heart flapping weakly in her breast. He stopped, only inches from her. She felt his heat and steeled herself against it, wishing with her very soul that she hadn't started all this. She should have known that his fiery Mediterranean ancestry harboured no leeway for forgiveness.

His breath, when he spoke, came with the heat of the devil, fanning her responses till she almost physically recoiled from him.

'I wonder if you are still such a bargain, or if perhaps life has finally taught you what honour is? I can't resist the temptation to try you out.' His voice was leaden with menace and his mouth so close to hers that it was almost touching. 'Don't kid yourself that it's a weakness on my part. One thing you taught me was never to let a little tease like you get under my skin again.'

Jade naïvely opened her mouth to form some sort of insult in retaliation, but her parted lips were given no chance to respond. They were suddenly claimed by his, hot and punishing and so shockingly sexual that all fight she might have summoned if forewarned disappeared for evermore.

His arms slid around her, crushing her to him just in case she thought of escape. Hard arms that had once melted her bones and melded her to him in the prelude to their passion. His mouth, scouring hers so painfully now, was a wicked reminder of the depth of feeling that had once charged between them. But then that feeling had had its roots in love and desire; now it was powered by the need for punishment.

Jade knew this and yet it made no difference to the aching need that Mel's kiss thrust into her unwilling heart. She didn't want to want him but she did. After all this time she still yearned for a small miracle to happen so that he would love her again. She wanted to tear herself away but couldn't. She knew she should be making some attempt to fight him but she couldn't.

She was utterly weak and senseless and she thought he must have sensed her submission. For one fleeting second she imagined his lips were softening. Was she willing the pressure to ease, to soften away from punishment and veer towards what they had once been to each other—passionate lovers?

She didn't know. The only thing she was sure of was that Mel Biaggio could still arouse her so deeply that she lost all control. And that must mean that he was still very much in her heart, and the thought was despairing and so very painful.

Her eyes were filled with tears of past regrets as she drew back from him, the first to move. So much loss and so much heartache to carry on living with. Where was the indifference she had hoped would take the place of her love after four years without sight of him?

He was completely unaffected by her look of despair, his eyes cold as his hands dropped to his sides.

Jade stared at him, determinedly now, the tears swallowed down hard and her eyes clear once again. She was the first to speak—bitingly, to hide the hurt.

'If I had thought you had sunk that low, Mel, I would never have dreamt of asking for your help. You came here today with no intention of even considering helping my company. Your sole purpose for being here is to insult me and humiliate me in revenge for what you think I did to you four years ago.'

He shook his head and his mouth twisted into a cruel half-smile. 'Revenge has nothing to do with my coming here today, Jade,' he grated roughly. 'And if you think that kiss was a punishment you are very wrong. What you think and feel is no concern of mine any more.'

There was nothing there, not a smidgeon of feeling for her, and it was irrational to be hurt but she couldn't ignore the pain that sliced through her.

'So why, Mel?' she cried impatiently. 'Why come here at all if it wasn't to make a fool of me?'

'I came here for my own selfish reasons,' he told her darkly. 'Something for me, nothing to benefit you, nothing to do with humiliation or insults or revenge.' His eyes suddenly narrowed and his jaw stiffened. 'I came here to lay a few ghosts of my past before I make the big commitment myself.'

He paused to let that sink in, a pause that homed in on its target—her heart—and then he added softly and yet lethally, striking where it hurt, 'Get my drift?'

Jade stared at him in horror, her dark eyes wide and brimming with pain. She was skidding on emotional black ice and couldn't stop. Her head was spinning. *Had* she got his drift, and was he...? Oh, so cruel, wicked even. She ran a tongue over dry lips before stuttering helplessly, 'Y-you're going to—to be married?'

There was a long, leaden silence before he responded. How clever he was at using those pauses to full effect. They were worse than words, the anticipation of what was to come the real cruelty.

'That's the drift,' he murmured at last. 'The ghosts of our past are firmly buried, Jade; and I'll tell you something—I'm glad, relieved, too. I've just one small regret. I'd have liked to think that by kissing you I might have aroused just a small measure of remorse in you for what we lost, because then I could have asked *you* how you felt about *my* betrothal.'

He turned then and Jade squeezed shut her smarting eyes against the pain, to close the world out. When she opened them the world was still spinning and Mel Biaggio was smiling at her from the open doorway—a cold, cynical smile. He held her file aloft.

'I'll take this with me. It'll make good bedtime reading. I'm a slave to insomnia. Hopefully, this should cure it.'

He slammed the door after him and shakily Jade sank into her chair and covered her face with her trembling hands. No, this couldn't be happening; she hadn't heard right, she hadn't got his drift and this was all too awful to bear. Mel, the great womaniser, had finally made a commitment to the woman he loved, and she, Jade Ritchie, *wasn't* that woman. Somehow it was so much worse knowing that his reputation had been grounded at last, because that must mean the lady in question was someone very special. Far more special than she had ever been to him. Oh, it hurt, so very much.

How irrational could you get? she asked herself in abject misery, because now she knew exactly how Mel had felt that night her father had announced her engagement to Nicholas. Totally, utterly betrayed and deeply hurt. And it was stupid, stupid, stupid, this awful feeling inside her, because he wasn't a part of her life any more. And yet he would be if he took her and her ailing company on. Everything was getting desperately worse instead of better...

CHAPTER TWO

JADE had her feelings of betrayal under control a few days later. How could she feel betrayed when she hadn't seen him for four years? But the truth was that she had never completely given up hope because he had always been in her heart. All the time she'd been reading about his latest amorous adventures with women in the gossip columns she'd allowed that hope to stay firmly implanted in her. Perverse as it might seem, she had thought that so long as he was womanising he wasn't finally lost to her. Now that he was about to be married, however, he definitely was. It was a thought she was trying to come to terms with and she was not having a whole lot of success. When you were dealt a devastating blow like that it wasn't easy to carry on as if the world was still turning.

'You're not cooking for me, are you?' Nicholas asked, coming up behind her in the kitchen part of the open-plan living area. 'I'm leaving for Paris almost immediately. The taxi will be here in a minute.'

'I know, I heard you ringing for it, and I'm not cooking, just heating up some canned soup. How long will you be away?'

'A couple of days. Did Mel Biaggio get in touch with you?'

Jade stirred the soup and gave a small sigh. 'Yes, while you were in Belgium. No go, I'm afraid. After looking at my financial statements he said I couldn't afford him.' She didn't tell him the content of the rest of their talk because Nicholas, being the sweetie he was, would show such concern that she'd be in tears before she knew it.

'Arrogant swine.'

'He has a point,' Jade said defensively. 'I'd have to mortgage this apartment to afford his fees.'

'Don't even think about it. I'll advance you the money.'

Jade turned to him, grinned and tweaked his chin. 'Your wedding money? Trisha would have a fit. She only tolerates you living here because I don't charge you rent and you can save quicker. Thanks for the offer, though; you're an angel. But it isn't the answer. I'm going to have to swallow my pride and—'

'Bargain with him?' Nicholas suggested with a thin smile.

'No way,' Jade retorted, and then sighed heavily. 'I'm going to have to tell Daddy. Hopefully he'll inject some money into the company and I'll struggle on.'

Nicholas took the wooden spoon from her, placed it on the counter, and put his hands on her shoulders. He was serious, worried about her. 'You said you couldn't bear the thought of facing him, and you know that isn't the answer anyway, Jade. In another year you'd be back in the same position and beholden to your father again. The company needs restructuring and you need financial advice too, and Mel Biaggio is the only one who can help.'

'Can't *you* help?' Jade pleaded softly, her limpid brown eyes wide and appealing. 'You could look over the books and—'

'I would have offered help before now if I thought I could be of service, but it isn't my field, Jade,' Nicholas insisted. 'Biaggio has the expertise. I wish I knew him personally; I'd have a word with him—'

The door buzzer went and Nicholas shrugged and let her go. 'That's the cab. I have to dash. Chin up, sweetheart. We'll talk about it when I get back.'

'Have a good trip,' she murmured as he went out of the door.

'I'm lonely,' she muttered to the soup. 'Resorting to talking to a pan of soup because there's no one special in my life. But once there was...'

Mel groaned as he gathered her lovingly into his arms, nuzzling her warm hair as they lay sprawled in the cornfield. A perfect day, a perfect picnic; everything was perfect.

'I hate parties,' he moaned. 'It'll mean I'll have to share you. Can't we just swish away on a magic carpet to somewhere romantic for your birthday? Paris would be perfect. The city of lovers.'

Jade giggled and twined his hair around her fingers. 'Daddy would never forgive you for whisking his baby away on her twenty-first. Besides,' she added, her voice low, seductive and teasing, 'you want to meet him, don't you? Haven't you something special you want to discuss with him?'

'Like his daughter's hand in marriage?'

He looked down at her, his eyes so full of love and adoration that her heart squeezed. He lowered his head and gently pulled at her lower lip with his teeth, murmuring, 'Do people still do that these days?'

'Not before they've made their intention quite clear to the lady in question,' she laughed.

He grinned down at her. 'Was that ever in dispute, my pocket-sized princess? I adored you from the moment I first set eyes on you queuing for bagels in Harrods food hall.'

'Doughnuts,' she corrected him and they both started to laugh, remembering how corny their first meeting had been. Jade had dropped her purse and her money had scattered; everyone had helped to gather it up and then, in the confusion, she had tried to pay with pesetas, not pounds, because she'd just come back from Spain. People had grown impatient and Mel had stepped in, paying for her and then gently taking her by the elbow and steering her out of the food hall and into his life.

'What ever happened to those doughnuts?' he murmured now as his mouth closed over hers in a kiss so deep and moving it was a perfect demonstration of how they felt about each other. Theirs was a wonderful, wonderful love, and they had a perfect future to look forward to.

She had every intention of introducing Nicholas to Mel at her twenty-first birthday party. They had been so wrapped up in themselves these past weeks that she hadn't considered her friends. Her father had organised a lavish party at their Kent home, Bankton House, as usual going over the top to compensate for Jade not having a mother.. Her mother had left when she was a small child, not able to live with John Ritchie's overbearing temperament a minute longer. Her father organised everyone's life. He did it the night of her party with disastrous results.

When Mel arrived she greeted him happily, but before she had a chance to whirl him around to meet her father and Nicholas another crowd of guests arrived.

He brushed a kiss across her hair. 'See what I mean? I'm having to share you. Come back soon, princess,' he teased, and then, with an understanding smile, he moved across the hall to the drawing-room buffet and bar. And that was where he was standing when John Ritchie got to his feet to make a speech Jade had known nothing about in advance. Her father opened his mouth and sent Jade's world crashing.

She caught the look of horror on Mel's face, but before she could reach him Nicholas clutched at her arm. He saw it as some sort of joke.

'Us, engaged to be married? Your father's drunk, surely?' He laughed.

Jade supposed Mel had witnessed Nicholas grasping her arm and laughing and assumed they were indeed a happy couple. Then, to make it worse, people surrounded her and Nicholas, offering congratulations and good wishes. Nicholas was laughing and spluttering, thinking it all a hoot, and by the time Jade could tear herself away Mel had disappeared. She found him getting into his Jaguar on the floodlit gravel drive, tearing his bow tie from the collar of his evening shirt.

'Mel!'

He turned, face gaunt and pale, eyes as hard as steel.

'Mel, you don't understand—'

'I understand you hadn't the courage to tell me to my face. You callous—'

'Please don't, Mel. You must listen. Nicholas and I—'

'Are engaged. Yes, I just heard. What sort of games are you playing, Jade?' He gave her no chance to answer before blazing on, 'God, what a fool you've made of me and what a character misjudgement I've made. You're nothing but a rich, spoilt child with no thought for people's feelings. You ...'

The chicken soup frothed over the side of the pan and Jade grasped it and hurled it into the sink. Tears streamed down her face just as they had the night she'd pleaded with Mel to listen to reason. She'd blurted that she and Nicholas were just good friends but even as she'd said

it she'd known it sounded hopelessly fragile. His Italian
ancestry made no allowances for boy-girl relationships
with no sexual undertones, but then Mel was a man of
the world—surely he could see that Nicholas wasn't a
threat to their relationship?

But of course she'd got nowhere with her reasoning
that fateful night. Mel had been too furious, too hurt,
too betrayed to listen. Until then he'd never heard of
Nicholas Fields and Jade knew she'd made a grave
mistake in not mentioning him before. Her only excuse,
not even voiced to Mel, was that their affair had been
so swift and intense that no one else had encroached on
their lives—not her father, not Nicholas, not anyone.

The phone rang, jarring her nerves, and Jade brushed
the tears from her face with the backs of her hands. She
knew it would be Trisha, wanting to know if Nicholas
had got off all right, and it was. Trisha's caring for
Nicholas only served to accentuate Jade's loneliness. She
envied what they had—a love, a life together, a future
full of promise. She forced herself to laugh and joke
with Trisha on the phone but her heart was heavy with
the emptiness of her life.

'Mel Biaggio has been ringing all morning,' Diane, Jade's
secretary, told her when she came in late after an un-
successful meeting with the company bank manager. He
could only offer so much, and it was not nearly enough.

Jade gazed at Diane in disbelief, her heart leaping
wildly. 'Mel Biaggio?' she breathed, slipping out of her
overcoat. 'Did he say what he wanted?'

Diane grinned ruefully. 'I did ask but he wouldn't say.
I told him you'd be in at lunchtime and he said he'd see
you then.'

Jade paled at the thought. He was coming here, just
when she had got herself together after his last visit. Had

he changed his mind about helping out? After all, he had taken the file with him. But perhaps he'd decided he hadn't punished her enough and was coming in for another stab at her!

She was ready for him when he arrived. Afraid but outwardly in control of her fear.

He crossed her office, tall, dark and maddeningly handsome, hardly looking at her as he approached. He tossed the file down on her desk. For a horrible second it occurred to Jade that the return of it was the only reason he was here.

'Th-thank you,' she murmured, eyeing him warily, wondering why he hadn't sent it by courier.

His face was expressionless as he spoke. 'I've given this a lot of thought and have a proposition to put to you.'

Jade widened her eyes. 'You've had a change of heart?' she uttered, and prayed her voice didn't sound too hopeful.

'Certainly not where you are personally concerned,' he clipped. 'I'd like to look over the place.'

Jade stared at him, smarting from his cold insult and puzzled by his request.

'Why?' she asked directly.

'I want to see what I'm letting myself in for,' he told her coldly.

Her heart didn't even miss a beat at the thought that he was considering taking the job on. His attitude dismayed her. He was so cold and clinical and once he hadn't been ... But they weren't lovers now and never would be again; this was business, and the only reason he was here, she reminded herself.

'So...so you think you can help?' He nodded. 'But why? Last week you said I couldn't afford you. Nothing's changed, Mel.'

'My thinking has,' he told her as he slid out of his cashmere coat and threw it down on a chair. 'Now, before I make a final decision are you going to show me around, or is my journey wasted?'

Jade steeled herself, and it was surprisingly easy now. This man before her wasn't the man she had loved so passionately. This Mel was different. He gave off not one scrap of warmth or sincerity. He was hard and unfeeling ... and was only here to do a job, she reminded herself yet again.

'Before I show you anything, Mel, you must make your intentions clearer,' she said formally. 'I've a lot to cope with at the moment and if this is your idea of more punishment for what happened between us forget it.'

'I won't forget it till the day I die,' he said coldly, his eyes intense. 'But that isn't why I'm here today. I pride myself on my professionalism and I don't think I gave you a fair hearing before.'

Jade's brows shot up in surprise. There was more to this than met the eye. 'Or perhaps you were thinking of your reputation,' she suggested knowingly.

He frowned. 'Meaning what?'

'Meaning word might have got around that you'd turned my company down because we were too small and ineffectual to promote your image as a high-flyer.' She couldn't resist that. It was very likely, too.

He smiled very thinly. 'I doubt you or any of your associates could harm my reputation or my image, Jade. You really are too small.'

She lifted her chin defiantly. 'Sometimes good things come in small packages—quantity isn't a guarantee of quality.'

He didn't say a word. His eyes locked onto hers and she felt mesmerised for a few seconds, then embarrassed when she got the message they were sending her. Small packages, pocket-sized princesses. Oh, she didn't want him here, looking at her like that, slamming their past at her with knowing looks.

She stretched taller, stiffened her shoulders, picked up a pen from the desk and thrummed it in her palm. 'I think you are wasting time, Mel—yours and mine. This isn't going to work out. There are other troubleshooters and—'

'They won't give you the time of day, Jade.'

'So what are you doing back here?' she burst out, rage welling inside her. Why couldn't he have stayed away? Oh, how she wished she had never involved him. It was awful, awful. 'You've no intention of giving your services. This is a personal vendetta and—'

'You were the one who called me in,' he challenged.

'Someone recommended you,' she argued. 'Because you're the best.' She cooled her tone but spiked it with sarcasm. 'In my opinion your best stinks. I wish I hadn't bothered—'

'So do I,' he sliced back at her. 'Because I can see trouble ahead all the way.'

'And with good reason. You've done nothing but put me down since stepping into my office and I don't have to take that—'

'Well, you'll have to get used to it because there's going to be plenty more where that came from,' he interrupted darkly.

'What do you mean?'

He stepped right up to her desk, leaned towards her and spoke levelly, his features, as usual, a mask of cold hostility. 'If I take this fiasco on I'm going to be breathing down your neck so hard you are going to need stabilisers to stay on your feet. I'm going to be digging so deep I'll rock your foundations. I'm going to be

probing every weakness and treading on every slack nerve
I find. Can you take that, I wonder?'

She glared at him in defiance. 'What exactly is that
supposed to mean? Are you talking about the ad agency
or was that a personal threat to *me*?'

His mouth thinned to a semblance of a smile. 'It boils
down to the same thing, Jade. You run this company so
every weak link leads back to you. I'll ask you again,
can you take it?'

Was there a choice? For a full half-minute she considered it, trying not to let her heart interfere and overrule
her sensibility. *Could* she take Mel breathing down her
neck, metaphorically or otherwise? There was no choice,
other than to face her father with her failure, and oddly
she'd rather face Mel. When this was over Mel would
be gone; her father was with her for life.

'Of course I can take it,' she fired back at him at last.
'I wouldn't have put up with all you've dished out to
me so far if I didn't want the best for the company and
my staff.'

'And what do you want for yourself out of all this,
if I decide to stay?' he asked heavily.

Her heart and soul cried out for what she truly wanted.
In spite of everything—his verbal brutality and
coldness—she wanted everything they had lost. The long,
hot summer and their love, the intensity of passion and
sweet pleasure of living each precious moment for each
other. But that wasn't possible. Mel was going to be
married and lost to her for ever. Jade took a deep, controlling breath and spoke with sincerity.

'I've failed my father's trust in me. I want to make
things right for the future of the company and for myself
I want peace of mind,' she told him slowly.

He looked at her long and hard before replying
smoothly, 'I wonder if you know what you do want,

Jade? I'm also beginning to wonder if your requesting my services has anything remotely to do with the business.'

Jade's mouth dropped open in astonishment and a fire scorched her spine at his veiled suggestion. Had she given something away—a look, a thought, a misplaced word? He couldn't think this was personal, surely? No, that was impossible—but then he did have some ego to nurture, she reminded herself. She forced a smile to cover her acute embarrassment.

'I wouldn't have you back if you came with a knighthood,' she told him disparagingly. 'You think you were the only one hurt that night, Mel. Your bigoted attitude damaged my love for you more than you could ever know.' Her eyes narrowed with anger. 'You gave me no space to explain. You wanted to believe it all because it was an easy way out for you. After all, your womanising ways weren't cultivated *after* we split up. You were born with them!'

'We were an excellent match, then, weren't we?' he grazed back at her sarcastically.

Her shoulders slumped in an unguarded second of defeat. How could she even begin to think that she could ever have any effect on him? He could hurt her so easily but her poisoned arrows hit an unyielding force, and because of that hostile defence of his she knew this could never work out. It was impossible for them to bury the past and channel their energies into getting her agency back on line.

'Yes, we were,' she agreed because it was the only way to be rid of him. Let them both think the worst of each other. 'And it's why this won't work. I thank you for your interest but it's not on.'

'My God, you're fickle,' he grated cynically. 'Is this why things have gone wrong here—because of your indecisiveness? You want my help, then you don't. Your back is against the wall, Jade. I'm your only saviour and you know it,' he informed her tightly.

'Yes, you are,' she acknowledged, inwardly agreeing that he had a point about indecisiveness. With him drawing the air from the room with his magnetism she couldn't stick to any firm decision. She couldn't think clearly any more. She had to, though. She had to force herself to *think*. Her dark eyes narrowed. 'But I might decide none of this is worth saving. I might decide bankruptcy has a nice ring to it as opposed to the ring of your insults in my ears!'

He smiled cynically. 'Bankruptcy is a painful state, sweetheart. Loss of kudos, status and very probably your home, your car and your valuables. I wonder if you could bear that?'

'You don't frighten me,' she returned, though her insides coiled tightly at the thought that he could think such things of her. 'But your arguments are a fair indication of what is important in *your* life: everything that pertains to materialism and ego,' she said bitingly. 'I wanted your help to save my employees more than my valuables, and, yes, my pride where my father is concerned.' She lifted her small chin. 'As an Anglo-Italian that might strike a chord with you. I've failed and I'm not afraid to admit it to you but my father is something else. He had faith in me and I failed him and...and I can't bear to face him.'

Oh, no, she could feel the tears flaming at the backs of her eyes. Damn him for exposing her vulnerability with such ease. She tossed the pen down on the desk, turned away from him and made for the door. She held it open, composed now, and defiant too. She'd cope, and without any help from him. She'd remortgage her flat, pawn her wretched valuables if it came to it. What she wouldn't do was humble herself to him any more!

'Actually, Mel Biaggio,' she said stoically, 'I owe you an enormous debt, but one I'm not going to offer any payment for. I'll take it as a freebie. Your insults and put-downs have served me very well. I'll fight this on my own if it's the last thing I do, just to prove to you I'm not that rich, spoilt child you keep insisting I am.'

She rapped her nails on the door to indicate that her patience was running thin and she would like him to leave. He made no movement, simply held her gaze with steely eyes as if wondering if she had it in her to struggle along on her own. Jade read the look and was more determined than ever. She'd do it, and on her own, too. Her fingers tightened round the edge of the door, willing him to hurry up and pass through it.

She smiled sweetly. 'Do let me know your wedding day, Mel, so I can send your intended my very best wishes . . . and sympathies,' she added meaningfully. If that didn't shift him nothing would, she thought.

Success. Slowly he moved towards her, without his coat. She parted her lips to remind him but he was upon her before she could utter a word. He took her arm and propelled her through the door. His grip on her was iron-hard and determined.

'You'll be the last to know my wedding date, sweet-heart,' he breathed, keeping his voice low because Diane was in the outer office. 'And now that I know you are determined to get this agency bouncing its merry little way along the road to success we'll get started.'

Once they were out in the corridor she breathlessly pulled her arm from his grip. Her cheeks were flaming as she swung to face him. He could talk of indecisiveness! He was the one who was up and down. So he was going to help, was he? If so, she wanted a promise from him to cool it, forget the past and get the job done. This was business and it needed to be separated from emotions. Emotions were draining.

She took a deep breath. 'There are conditions—'

The laughter that cut her off wasn't fired by humour. 'I make the conditions, sweet one, and you just do as you're told.'

Gritting her teeth, without another word Jade turned away from him and led the way to the stairwell, her stomach churning. Grit and bear it, not even grin and bear it, was going to be her motto from now on. It was all quite unbearable but she had no choice but to put up with it. Halfway up the stairs to the next floor, in control again, her emotions buried deep inside her, she spoke.

'Administration's on my floor, the studio above,' she told him without looking at him.

'Just the two floors?'

'This is Soho, not the Sahara,' she told him flintily. 'The rents are astronomical around here.'

'Perhaps that's where you're failing—not thinking big enough,' Mel parried.

'Perhaps I know my capabilities and live within them,' she retorted sharply.

He made no comment but held the swing door open for her. Her arm brushed his as she passed through. Both were adequately clothed, Jade in a cherry-red suit, the jacket cut in sharply to accentuate her tiny waist, and Mel in a Savile Row creation in silver-grey, but she felt the contact as acutely as if they had both been naked. Her eyes flicking up to his, she wondered if he had been as aware of the contact as she had. His leaden eyes gave nothing away and she despised herself for her own recollection of times long gone when any touch, however slight, had sparked thrillingly between them.

She paused in the tiny foyer outside the studio before entering. Nodding towards the glass doors through which you could see the whole layout of the floor, she told him, 'As you can see, some of the boards are vacant. I've got three key staff off with a flu bug.'

'Let's hope you don't go down with it, then. It only takes a kiss for these things to spread like the plague.'

His eyes were gleaming with mockery as he said it and he was standing close enough for an infectious kiss. Jade didn't know why that thought had even occurred to her when she was still wondering if that was another stab at her supposed loose morals of four years back. Whatever, she warded him off with her own preventative remedy— biting sarcasm.

'You're in for a chronic overdose of whatever's doing the rounds, then,' she retorted tartly, turning her back on him to push open the inner door of the studio, his low, not madly amused laughter making the hairs on the back of her neck prickle.

She showed him around the studio, thinking how jaded it all looked when you were forced to see it through someone else's eyes. New equipment was needed, new enthusiasm, an injection of fresh spirit. Jade stood on the sidelines, listening to what Mel had to say and not interfering but resenting the enthusiasm and keenness he seemed to be drawing from her all-male artistic staff. She supposed word had got round that things weren't going terribly well in the company and they saw Mel Biaggio's interest as something positive. If Mel agreed to help she'd have to inform them that he was a trouble-shooter and there would be inevitable changes.

'Every one of them needs a kick in the rear,' he told her sourly as they concluded their tour of inspection, Mel holding the door open for her, Jade avoiding brushing against him again.

She swallowed his contempt and kept her objections to herself. He'd warned her what to expect and she'd have to take it or face the consequences. She was learning but it wasn't easy.

'Who occupies the ground floor of the building?' Mel asked as they returned to the first floor, where the offices were. Jade led him through the main open-plan office, and it was obvious that most of the female staff were stunned at the sight of Mel, tall, charismatic and God's gift to the young and nubile.

'It's vacant at the moment,' she told him.

He said nothing till they were back in her office and then he shot the lot at her, taking her breath away with his suggestions.

'You have to be joking!' she protested hotly. This was ridiculous. 'I can't afford to expand. How can I take on another floor when I can scarcely raise the rent for two? As for taking on more staff, there's scarcely enough work for the ones I've got after that creep creamed off my best clients.' She was almost trembling with rage. This was his revenge once again. His suggestions were crazy. If she took them up ruin would slap her in the face sooner rather than later. Was that his intention? To take his revenge to the very end—total destruction?

His eyes darkened at her protestations. 'You can't get any lower than you already are, Jade. There's only one way out of this situation and that is up. Now, if you are scared of the challenge quit now, because you're no good to me if you don't think positively. You'll need financing and I can help; you'll need new contacts and I'll help. I can put key staff in here who will inject new enthusiasm . . .'

In awe Jade listened to it all, acknowledging the power and energy the man had and realising why he was so successful. She felt her spirits lift for her company but still a deep part of her lamented her emotional loss. She knew she shouldn't even be considering her own feelings when he was outlining plans for saving her company but she couldn't help the snap of sorrow squeezing at her heart. With all these changes going on he would be around a lot. Would she be able to cope with the sight of him? With the knowledge that every day was bringing him closer to his wedding day—the day when she would know for sure it was finally over?

Mel picked up his coat from the chair. 'I'll turn this company around in three months,' he told her at last.

'And...and your price?' she uttered weakly, still dazed by his restructuring plans.

Slowly he came across the thick carpet to her, something so strange in his eyes that she steeled herself. The crunch was about to come, she sensed, some exorbitant fee that would cancel out any profits that might come from his new plans for the company.

After folding his coat over one arm, his hand came up to grip her chin quite firmly. His touch was paralysing, numbing her limbs and yet making her nerve-endings tingle. His dark, broody eyes captured hers so utterly compellingly that she had no choice but to stare at him, wide-eyed.

'At the end of three months, if not before, you'll know my price, sweetheart,' he said in a dark undertone which made his words sound more like a threat than anything else. 'But don't ever forget I don't come cheap.'

Jade ran the feverish tip of her tongue over her lower lip—the lip he was scorching with his eyes. She felt danger shiver down her spine. It was the way he was looking at her...as if...as if he wanted to claim those lips.

'I'll pick you up at nine,' he breathed softly. 'Dinner and more discussions before we get this rolling.' She opened her mouth to protest. 'Don't argue,' he cut in before she could. 'I've warned you. Just remember I always know best.'

He left her suffering yet another indignity, which washed over her like a tidal wave. The indignity of not having any choice but to put up with his arrogant pomposity. No, Mel Biaggio didn't come cheap. She would pay the price all right, more than she could have envisaged at the outset of all this. In fact she had started the instalments already. She was going to pay dearly for ever having fallen in love with him.

CHAPTER THREE

JADE had already decided she wouldn't invite him up to the apartment when he arrived. He'd buzz and she'd be ready and she'd tell him over the intercom she was on her way down. She wasn't going to allow him into her space, to suffer him looking around critically and making disparaging remarks about her lifestyle, which she was sure he would, just to be unpleasant.

He saved her the trouble when he buzzed and said to hurry down as he had the engine running. It was precisely nine o'clock. He couldn't have been more on the dot if he'd been the keeper of Big Ben.

Jade took one last look at herself in the mirror. Why had she bothered to make herself look special? she wondered. Was it for him or just for her own self-esteem? She felt so tight inside, she wasn't at all sure about her reasons for anything any more. She wore a clingy black velvet dress softened with a cream and peach silk scarf around her throat. Her heels were the highest she could stagger in. They were making a comeback after flatties being in fashion for so long. She'd always worn risky heels with him, though, he being so tall, she so small.

Her eyes were misty as she hurriedly slicked on another coat of red lipstick. She'd nervously drawn on her lips so much that there was hardly any colour left. As she'd got ready the past had flooded her, bringing with it the despair of her loss yet again. She'd loved dressing up for him when they were lovers. It had all been a ritual, everything done for his pleasure and approval. He'd adored her femininity, laughed at her feisty temper when aroused, hungered for her kisses. Now he despised her so openly that she dreaded facing him again, and yet here she was, checking and rechecking her appearance, and what for? More painful put-downs?

The last thing she did before turning away from the mirror was to harden her heart against him, pride adding to the steely determination. She looked the way she did for self-preservation, not his approval.

'Why dinner, Mel? I'm sure we could have done all this in my office some time.' Chin up, she settled into the passenger seat of his black BMW and he pulled away from the kerb. It was pouring with rain, with a biting wind to add to the misery of the winter night.

'I don't have *some time*, Jade. You're not the only poor fish in the sea of troubled waters these days.'

'How very poetic,' Jade muttered. Then she drew in her breath as almost immediately they pulled up outside a restaurant they both knew very well from the past. This was a bit below the belt and she felt the blow as if it had been physically thrown. 'Was it worth it?' she snapped. 'We could have walked around the corner.'

'You, in those ridiculous heels?' he said, opening his door and getting out.

He'd never disapproved of them before, she thought miserably, and supposed his woman wore designer trainers.

Jade made no further comment on his choice of venue as he put a steadying arm around her shoulders and they hurried into the crowded restaurant. She made no comment as the waiter ushered them to the same window seat they used to occupy, obviously requested by Mel to make her feel bad. She did comment on the change of view, however, to hide her floundering emotions and the deadly beat of her aching heart.

'Didn't that used to be a pizza house across the road?' She hoped she sounded light and casually interested instead of desperately unhappy, which she was. This was his revenge, bringing her here to stir up old memories.

'Looks like a Thai restaurant now,' Mel said, leaning forward to peer through the window. 'I've not been back since we split up,' he added, so matter-of-factly that Jade knew none of this meant anything to him any more.

But why should it? He'd found love elsewhere and four years had passed anyway. She gazed miserably at the menu. Naturally it had changed over the years but there was nothing on it to bring her appetite back. She ordered fish and he followed suit and then she got down to business immediately, ignoring the twisting inside her as women gazed at the back of Mel's head, probably wondering what a gorgeous man like him was doing out with a little nobody like her.

As Mel spoke Jade listened and drew herself out of her self-pity, raising her chin and squaring her shoulders as one of a group of businessmen across the room gave her a very interested look. It was as if Mel suddenly had psychic powers. He turned and caught the man looking and then gave her a withering look.

'You haven't changed, have you?' he said pityingly.

'Is that a serious question?' she demanded tightly.

'Rhetorical.'

'Abysmal, Mel, like your thinking. I wasn't flirting. If you must know I was sitting here feeling very sorry for myself and wondering how far I had sunk in these last years to end up dining with you, and then that good-looking young man gave me an encouraging look and I responded because he made me feel attractive and alive and not the total waste of time you obviously think I am.'

He said nothing for a while, just twirled his water glass in his fingers as he studied it with equal intensity. When he did finally speak his words made her uncomfortable in her seat.

'After all these years I still want to punch the jaw of any man who looks at you.'

She recovered quickly. 'I doubt that. You'd rather punch *my* jaw, as you symbolically did by thinking I was two-timing you four years ago. You haven't changed either, Mel,' she finished contemptuously.

The waiter brought them wine and Mel studied her across the table as she sipped hers. 'I think we'd better keep to business before we upset each other any more,' he suggested at last.

'Honesty upsets you, does it?' Jade couldn't resist taunting.

'Stop it, Jade,' he warned. 'It isn't funny and it isn't sensible if I'm going to be involved in your daily business.'

He was right, of course. She remembered his warning: 'Don't argue'. She might as well have her tongue stitched to the roof of her mouth and be done with it.

'You were saying something about putting in a new head of the art department,' she started, determined to get all this over and done with so that she could go home and curl up in misery on the sofa for the rest of the night.

'Yes, I have someone very talented who would fit the bill.'

Jade braced herself. 'Mel, I know you said I wasn't to argue, so don't take this as arguing, take it as a statement of fact. My problems aren't with the art department. The staff I have are very talented. I've fallen down in other departments and that is where I need your advice.'

'You need a new art director,' he insisted.

Jade held her palms up to him. 'I'm not arguing, honest, but I have enough talent to promote someone within my own staff without bringing in someone from outside.'

He glowered at her. 'If that isn't arguing, I don't know what is.'

Jade sighed. 'You can't expect me to lie down and take it all without giving an opinion.'

He'd obviously expected exactly that. His eyes narrowed, daring her to say another word.

'OK.' She sighed again and drew in a last defiant breath. 'If you must you must, but I can't afford to take a risk with some fresh-faced kid just out of art school who thinks he's going to change the face of advertising with a working model of a Lamborghini made out of cornflake packets!'

To her astonishment he burst out laughing and his amusement cut right through her till she almost winced with pain. Their affair might have been short and explosive but they had lived and loved and laughed so very much and how she had missed him, so very, very much.

He refilled their wineglasses, still shaking his head. Jade watched him with stinging eyes and a heart that felt as if it was pounding its last beats. What a waste, what a loss, what a fool she had been not to *force* him to listen that night.

'It's a she, not a he,' he said after putting the wine bottle back into the ice bucket.

The waiter brought their main course and Jade waited till he'd gone before asking, 'Who is a she, not a he?'

'Your new art director.'

A chill went down Jade's spine. Knowing his tabloid reputation with the opposite sex, *she* was sure to have had an intimate relationship with him at one time. *She*

might be *his* she! No, his fiancée certainly wouldn't need
to earn her own living.

'The boys aren't going to like that!' Jade exclaimed.
All her art staff were men because the few women they
had tried couldn't keep up the pace.

'That sounds sexist.'

Jade shrugged and gave a small smile. 'I suppose it
does but I'm not sexist. Give me a girl who can stand
the pace and won't get pregnant and I'll take her on.'

'That is definitely sexism,' Mel insisted.

Her smile broadened. 'I was quoting my father, actually. You know, the one with the big mouth and the
Draconian temperament?'

'I never got around to the pleasure of meeting him,'
Mel grazed, and fixed her with an icy glare that wiped
the smile from her mouth and brought a flush to her
cheeks.

She shouldn't have mentioned her father and, worse,
tried to make a joke of him. Her intention had been to
lighten the atmosphere between them but she had failed
miserably, her choice of subject appalling under the circumstances. She regretted it deeply.

'And I can personally guarantee that Nadia won't get
pregnant,' Mel added with such conviction that it was
like another whiplash to her senses.

Jade stared down at her fish, feeling as limp and as
lifeless as the poor thing sprawled on her plate. He could
only make a guarantee like that if he was very heavily
involved. This Nadia *was* his intended, the woman he
loved, the woman he was going to spend the rest of his
life with. And Mel Biaggio was about to install her at
the heart of her company!

She tried to swallow but it was impossible. She was
so choked up she thought she might as well roll over and
die right now. She would never be able to cope with

having this Nadia thrust at her from all sides. It was
cruel and wicked and he knew exactly what he was
doing—punishing her. But for it all to be effective he
must think she still cared because there would be no point
otherwise.

Nervously she reached for her wineglass. He must
never know how she still felt about him. Never, but never
would she allow him to have any idea that he was getting
to her.

She smiled, forcing normality and genuine interest into
her tone. She forced courage into her heart, too. 'This
Nadia woman. Is she the one—the one who is going to
end your womanising ways?'

'What do you think?' His eyes were clear and unyielding and Jade thought she read cruelty in them. He
was enjoying this, hoping he was getting to her.

'I suppose she must be,' she sighed wearily. And he
had verbally guaranteed her childless state for the time
being, obviously not ready for a family yet. Oh, it didn't
bear thinking about. She swallowed, fighting to sound
normal. 'Tell me about her. Do you really think she'll
be able to turn things around?'

'She'll be able to bring her own clients...'

Jade concentrated hard. This was awful—discussing
his mistress joining her company. She wanted to walk
out of the restaurant after telling him what to do with
his help and advice, but then he would know she still
cared and couldn't face it. She took a deep breath.

'I don't want her if she's going to poach from the
company she's working with now. I've had a taste of
that, don't forget. It would be wrong.'

'She's freelance...'

He went on to extol her talents till Jade's head was
whirling with them and unwelcome jealousy tugged miserably at her heart. Apparently she was an award-winner

for a series of television ads she'd done for a string of hotels, and headhunters were queuing up with offers from here and abroad. Quite a high-flyer in the advertising world, it seemed.

This Nadia had so much going for her that Jade wondered what was behind Mel's putting her into her little ad agency. Surely such a talent wouldn't consider working for such a small set-up without good reason? The good reason must be her love for Mel. He probably didn't want his intended stretching her talents very far from him and Jade's little agency would be a suitable place for her till they got married.

Deep depression and regret settled around Jade's shoulders like a ton weight. Suddenly overwhelmed with fatigue at the coffee stage, she murmured, 'You've given me a lot to think about, Mel. I'll walk myself home. I need some air.'

'It's still raining,' he said. 'I'll drive you.' He stood up and settled the bill and Jade waited, too tired to argue. She gazed out of the window and wished herself away in some foreign part, as far away from Mel Biaggio as possible. Somewhere like South America would do nicely. But it was too late now. He was going to be a part of her company's recovery and things had gone too far for her to stop it.

'Thanks,' she murmured some ten minutes later as he pulled up outside her apartment block. 'I won't ask you up for coffee.'

'I wouldn't come,' he told her, leaning across her to open the passenger door. He grasped the scarf at her throat before she had a chance to step out of the car. He held it firmly, slowly twisting it around his fingers, tightening it, drawing her closer to him. 'I have someone warm and willing waiting at home for me,' he taunted in a smooth, seductive drawl, his breath warm on her mouth. As further punishment he pressed his lips to hers and scoured them thoroughly, a physical way of showing her just what she was missing. It sent her pulses thrashing crazily, destroying her very soul.

She let him take his fill and she didn't allow a scrap of emotion to break through and give him any satisfaction. She was stiff and unyielding under his pressure, struggling to hold onto her defiance under devastating provocation. He'd never know—he couldn't know how hard her heart beat, how close she was to sobbing out his name against his lips and throwing her arms around his neck and clinging to him.

He drew back at last and in the street lighting she could just see the gleam of anger in his eyes. He was mad at her for not showing any signs of arousal but she felt no triumph, just a terrible thrumming of her heart at the cold, calculated way he showed no emotion other than anger. The kiss really had meant nothing to him; it had merely been a reprisal.

She smiled at him. 'And I have someone warm and willing waiting for me too,' she lied sweetly, and got out of the car.

Before she could slam the door in his face he called out, 'Enjoy your cocoa, darling.'

Boiling with rage, Jade let herself into the apartment block. He couldn't have known that cocoa was *exactly* the warm and willing 'someone' waiting for her. Once inside her apartment she did what she had longed to do all evening—curled up on the sofa with her misery for company. . . and her cocoa.

Remarkably Jade's depression lifted after a few days. To give him his due, Mel Biaggio was a wizard. Without him even putting in another personal appearance something magical had happened within the company.

Enthusiasm. Though the wicked fairy, in the form of Nadia, hadn't appeared either, word had got around that she was joining the company and expectations were high. Because of Mel the bank manager was suddenly tripping over himself to help and a lease was being drawn up to secure the ground floor for a further studio and presentation room. Mel Biaggio moved in amazing ways.

The following Monday morning Jade threw herself into her work with greater enthusiasm than normal. Her adrenalin was still flowing as fast as a rising tide when she lifted the phone during Diane's lunch break. It was Mel, and on recognising his voice her heart twisted and she wished it wouldn't do that. She was coping, she really was.

'Where are you?' she asked, twisting her pen in her free hand.

'Rome. I'm sorry I've left you to it these last few days but my schedule is tight. How is Nadia doing?'

Jade raised a brow. 'Doing what?' she replied drily.

'Settling in.'

'Since she hasn't put in an appearance yet it's hard to say,' was Jade's sarcastic retort. She would have thought he'd know.

She heard a small groan from Mel. 'What time is it over there?'

Anyone would think he was on another planet instead of just in Italy, she thought wryly. She glanced at her watch. 'Ten past one.'

Mel sounded concerned. 'She doesn't usually rise till about ten, but...'

Her heart shredded. She didn't want to know about their personal life.

'But what?' Jade couldn't help urging. Nadia's sleeping habits really were no concern of hers but this was affecting the business.

'But she knew she was supposed to be starting with you this morning. She sounded fine on the phone last night.' He sounded miles away, more than land miles. He *sounded* deeply concerned. 'I'd better ring her right away.'

Jade wondered what sort of a relationship they had, because if they were love's sweet dream wouldn't he have rung her first thing in the morning? As he used to ring her when they were lovers, eager to hear her voice on waking.

'Well, when you finally drag her out of bed, Mel,' she told him frostily, 'tell your prima donna we start rehearsals at nine sharp every morning and if she can't make it she's out before she's in!'

With that Jade slammed down the phone, and immediately bitterly regretted it. Her vitriol only proved one thing—that she was jealous. But hopefully he wouldn't see it that way. Hopefully he would think she was in business mode this morning and feeling very frustrated that Nadia was holding up the recovery of her company.

Nadia didn't show up the following day, or Wednesday, and by Thursday Jade had given her up for good. So much for Mel's grandiose ideas about branching out into the lucrative world of television commercials.

He walked into her office on Friday morning, taking Jade by surprise. She hadn't known he was back in the country.

'Nadia is down with the flu,' he told her, loosening his tie as he crossed the room to her desk. 'That's why she hasn't put in an appearance.'

'She could have phoned,' Jade said drily. She tensed her knees under her desk. So could he, come to that. He must have known on Monday that she was ill.

'Nadia is a bit vague with telephone numbers, and besides, the poor darling is really quite sick.'

'I'm sorry,' Jade felt obliged to say, though she wasn't convinced that flu could have made her so sick as to render her incapable of making a phone call. A bad memory for numbers was no excuse. I'm being picky, Jade decided, driven by this devil here showing concern for his 'poor darling'.

'Anyway, I apologise on her behalf and I'm sure she'll be on her feet in next to no time.'

Jade watched him thoughtfully as he sat down and picked up her phone as if this were his office, his phone, his business. He looked so serious, but then did she expect him to look otherwise? Nadia, the woman he loved, was unwell and he had committed himself and Nadia to helping her company and was probably regretting it as much as she, Jade, was.

In the confines of her small office, with the door shut and a miserably cold, bleak London day pressing at the windows, she was claustrophobically aware of his physical presence: tall, hard and muscular, severe now as he concentrated on his call. She could even smell him—the same cologne he always used. She could almost feel his silky hair under her fingertips. She trembled inwardly and got up, and was standing at the window when he clicked the phone down.

'Shall we get on, then?' he suggested, his voice surprisingly gravelly.

Jade turned in time to see him watching her intently, with an expression of... She tried to analyse the look quickly. Was it regret? Perhaps longing, if she stretched her imagination to its limits. She lowered her eyes. Imagination hurt.

'Yes,' Jade said, after taking a steadying breath and lifting her chin. 'I must take advantage of you while

you're here . . .' Colour rose to her cheeks and she gave
a half-smile which he returned. 'You know what I mean,'
she added hurriedly.

'Yes, I do,' he murmured back.

Her imagination hummed again. Had she detected
regret in his tone? Was she looking for and expecting
something that was impossible? She was hopelessly out
of line, she decided, going to her desk and picking up
some papers she wanted him to go over with her. He
was committed to someone else, he loved someone else.
There was nothing in his heart for her any more.

'I've had enough,' Jade breathed wearily as they came
back into her office after a lengthy tour of the ground
floor, Mel having secured the keys at some time. He
overwhelmed her with his drive but then she supposed
he was fed by a need to get the company running so that
he could get out of her life as quickly as possible. But
with Nadia working here would he ever be completely
out of her life? The thought prompted a question.

'If your Nadia ever shows up, how long do you think
she'll stay? I mean, the purpose is for her to help boost
our output. If and when it's ticking over nicely, is she
going to leave?'

She poured coffee from the pot at the small courtesy
bar built in a corner of her office and waited for his
answer. What she was really asking was when they intended getting married, because she was sure Mel
wouldn't want a working wife.

'We'll cross that bridge when we come to it,' was his
evasive answer.

Jade felt cheated as she handed him a cup of coffee.
She hadn't even had to ask how many sugars he took,
or if he preferred cream or milk or black. She remembered it all. Hot, bitter and black, very much like his
moods now.

'I would like to know,' Jade gently insisted, hoping she didn't sound too pushy.

'Why?'

'Because,' she said, an edge to her tone this time, 'I want to know where I stand. If she's so wonderful and works a miracle here—'

'I'm the one working miracles, Jade; remember that.' He leaned back against her desk and drank his coffee, all cool sophistication.

'You won't let me forget,' she muttered as she slumped down in her father's old leather office chair and glared at him.

'It's not as bad as I thought it might be,' he said. 'It won't take much to swing it all around.'

'The company, you mean?' she said absently, taking a furtive glance at her watch. It was nearly six, the staff had left and she wanted out too. She was driving down to the country for the weekend and wanted to get going. She'd had to cope with so much this week and exhaustion was clawing at her. She wanted peace and quiet and time to rest and recharge her batteries because next week with him would be much the same—emotionally draining.

'Are you interested?' he suddenly asked, and her head shot up to meet his hard gaze.

'Yes, I'm interested.'

His eyes narrowed threateningly. 'Well, pay attention, Jade, and stop looking at your watch. I can see how you've let things slide—'

'That's not fair, Mel,' she interrupted flintily. 'I did not willingly let things slide. I took a knock with those poached clients and it's entirely due to my hard work that I didn't go all the way down. Don't talk to me as if I'm a child and you're a school master. You're too pedantic by far.'

Impervious to her anger, he asked coolly, 'Why the eagerness to get away? Is someone waiting for you?'

She eyed him coldly. He sure knew how to put the knife in and twist it cruelly. 'I wouldn't tell you if there was, Mel. Suffice to say I'm going down to the country for the weekend.'

He frowned disapprovingly. 'Is a cosy weekend in the country a wise move when all is chaos around you here at the moment?'

Heavens, was he planning on working all weekend when he'd hardly shown his face all week? If so he was utterly unreasonable. She looked around the office, which was pristine after Diane had tidied up before leaving.

'I see no chaos,' she drawled, picking up her coffee-cup and taking it and his to the sink to rinse them.

'Sarcasm doesn't suit you, Jade, and ruin won't either if you don't work with me to get things moving here.'

She turned on him, bitterly angry at the injustice of that remark. She'd worked herself into the ground this week and was suffering for it now, with exhaustion. 'Mel Biaggio, I wasn't the one swanning around Rome this week and I'm not the "poor darling" in bed with the flu. I've been here all week, bursting a few blood vessels, and if you think I've been doing less than nothing to help myself you might as well go now and leave me to the ruin you are forever wishing on me!'

She was so angry, her nails scored into her palms as she clenched her fists at her sides. At every opportunity he was goading her. It was unbearable and she couldn't take much more.

She saw his body stiffen and then he came to her and gripped her narrow shoulders. 'I don't swan around anywhere, Jade,' he rasped. 'It's been a tough week all round and it's going to get tougher. This isn't the time for weekends in the country.'

The pressure of his hands burned into her shoulders. Why was he always angry with her, why was he always so angry and bitter? She jerked away from him and grabbed at the tea-towel to dry the cups—anything to distance herself from him.

'Go home, Mel,' she said through tight lips. 'Someone warm and willing is waiting for you. Have a good weekend.'

She heard him sigh impatiently. 'We need to be here, Jade,' he grated from behind her. 'There are a million and one things to be sorted out. I have other clients and—'

'No, Mel,' she insisted firmly, her back to him. It wasn't necessary, surely—this overtime, this urgency? If the truth be known she was so stressed out she couldn't face another hour, let alone the weekend.

'I have to go down to Bankton House this weekend,' she went on. 'I go once a month to see that the house is still standing. My father only gets back from France twice a year.' She shut up. He wasn't interested unless it affected his schedule.

'And what do you do there all weekend—hole up with your latest lover?' he asked in a low, level voice.

She swung round, hating him for that. Her whole body tensed with anger and hurt. If she'd been big enough and had the strength she'd have slapped his jaw for stabbing at her morals yet again.

'That was totally out of order, Mel,' she seethed. 'If I hole up with twenty lovers it's none of your business. I resent your unwarranted assaults on my privacy. I don't probe into your love life so leave mine alone.'

He stepped towards her and grasped her shoulders again, and just before he kissed her he murmured throatily, 'I wish I *could* leave your love life alone.'

His mouth on hers drew the very worst from her—a need so compelling and demanding that she felt dizzy with it. His arms held hers at her sides in case she thought of struggling free, but that would have been impossible anyway. She couldn't move. Mesmerised, she suffered the sweet pressure, and as the kiss deepened and tugged at her senses for a response she knew the agony would never end. She thought of all those wasted years spent trying to forget him, knowing now that her efforts had been futile.

In a dazed state she wondered what was going through his mind and then, in a rush of sudden awareness, she knew. No regrets for him. This was another test of endurance for her. He was giving her the chance to prove whether the remarks she'd thrown at him about lovers were true. If she had so many why didn't she give herself to him, as she had so willingly a lifetime ago?

Love, hate, fury. They all balled inside her, lending her strength and clearing her head. She shrank back from him, her eyes as cold and as unfeeling as the ones staring down at her now.

'You did well to pin my arms at my sides, Mel Biaggio,' she seethed through white lips. 'I might have inflicted damage on you you would have found difficult to explain to your lover.'

His eyes held hers daringly. He let go of her arms and held his hands up in case she didn't believe she was free. It was also a gesture of temptation. Would she carry out her threat?

'You're not worth it,' she grated contemptuously, clenching her fists at her sides.

'Nor you, sweetheart,' he said as he dropped his hands away from her.

'So why, Mel?' she pleaded heatedly. 'Why do you say the things you do—hateful things intended to hurt me? Why do you kiss me? Is it to punish me more?'

His eyes gleamed, metallic and cruel, and his jawline was as taut as barbed wire. 'I kissed you for the same reason as the first time—to lay some ghosts. Trouble is, sweetheart, you are proving some heavyweight ghost to exorcise. Perhaps the solution would be your total submission. Perhaps then I'd be able to get on with my life and not see your face and body every time I lie with another woman!'

With one last demonic look he turned away, slammed the office door after him, leaving Jade trembling at the brutality of his words. Their meaning sank into her dazed mind slowly, poisonously. He wanted more than a kiss to exorcise their past. He wanted her total submission and only then would his appetite for revenge be sated.

Oh, God, what had she started, and what could she do to escape this terrible punishment he wanted to inflict on her? She wouldn't be able to stand it, to live through this crippling torment. But he'd said 'perhaps'—perhaps he'd change his mind.

Jade hugged herself for comfort and stared up at the ceiling, biting hard on her lower lip. The trouble was, she knew Mel Biaggio. Once he had an idea in his mind the devil himself couldn't shift it. He'd try and carry out his threat but the outcome lay with her. She wouldn't allow him to destroy her as he intended. She had to be strong and she would be. She was a survivor. He wouldn't win. Ever.

CHAPTER FOUR

MEL BIAGGIO had given Jade a headache never to forget. Her forehead throbbed as she drove down the motorway, wishing she had stayed in London for the weekend where it was warmer. Flurries of snow covered the windscreen and she switched on the wiper-blades, comforting herself with the thought that by going down to Bankton House and running the central heating for a few days she would prevent the water pipes freezing up. This was therapy, she decided. Occupying herself down at the house would blot out the turmoil of what Mel was putting her through. She'd clean and polish and positively *not* allow herself to think.

She wondered if she was too late to save the plumbing when she entered the old Victorian house on the edge of the Kentish village she had grown up in. It was perishingly cold and she shivered uncontrollably as she snapped on the central heating boiler in the kitchen and then went around switching lamps on, which at least created an image of warmth.

Hunched with cold, she paused in the vast drawing room. Every time she came in here she could see the spectre of Mel standing across the room as he had done the night of her party, stunned, face white and drawn after hearing her father make that appalling engagement announcement.

She turned away, hugging her arms around her, tears pricking her eyes. If only she could turn the clock back and do it right this time, somehow blot out her father and Nicholas... She wondered how many people in the

world had wished that on themselves—to go back and
try again. It was impossible, of course. No one had such
power and some would say you could learn by your mistakes, but all she had learned was that she still had
feelings for Mel, feelings with nowhere to go.

She needed something warm and willing—a hot cup
of cocoa then bed and sleep to deaden those punishing
thoughts of Mel that were hurting her so badly.
Resolutely she closed the drawing-room door and went
to the kitchen, where it was so cold and miserable that
she abandoned the thought of cocoa and went straight
upstairs to bed, wishing she hadn't come.

She awoke in the middle of the night, muddled, not
sure where she was, shivering and yet feverish, as if she'd
had a bad dream. There was an eerie silence and her
throat raged with thirst. She groped her way up from
under the duvet to get a drink, and by the time she
reached the bathroom she knew she was coming down
with something.

'Flu,' she groaned feebly, feeling for the radiator and
dismayed to find it stone-cold. The taps yielded no water.
She jumped nervously as an icy wind whipped the bare
branches of a tree against the bathroom window. Already
there were inches of snow piled against the sill.

In despair Jade realised there was no water because
the pipes were already frozen and that for the same
reason there was no central heating. Her head reeled with
frustration. She'd have to call a plumber first thing in
the morning and then drive back to London. If she was
going to be ill let it be in warmth and comfort rather
than this. But for now all she wanted to do was go back
to bed and pull the duvet over her throbbing head.

As she staggered back to her cold bedroom, feeling
achy and wretched, her sympathies winged to Nadia of
all people. She understood now how the other woman

must have felt when the bug had hit her, appreciated that she probably had been too weak to pick up the phone. It was all Jade could do to pull the duvet over her.

'Mel!' Jade cried. She tried to move her head but it felt as if it was in a vice. Why was she crying Mel's name? She didn't want him, she didn't need him...

'Lie still. Try and drink this.'

Jade blinked open her eyes and then squeezed them shut again. The room had spun and the light had burned her eyes. She tried to turn over to slide out of bed but the bed was floating.

'Jade, sweetheart, stop thrashing and try and drink this.'

She felt her head being lifted and a warm lemony drink being held to her lips. Jade swallowed and coughed and swallowed some more.

'Darling, listen; I'm going to try and dress you and take you away from here.'

'I can't, she moaned weakly. 'It's too cold.'

'I know,' the voice whispered close to her face. 'That's why I want to get you away. There's no heating or water...'

The voice trailed away and Jade drifted into sleep again, feeling hot and cold and dizzy and weak. Later she lifted her heavy eyelids to find that the brightness had gone and there was darkness at the window. The darkness moved and came towards her. She looked up and saw that the darkness was Mel.

'Still feeling awful?' he breathed with concern.

He was bending over her, his dark hair falling across his creased forehead, eyes dark and worried, his mouth drawn into a tight line. Mel was here but he couldn't be real. Was he an image conjured up by her fever? Her hand floated up to touch the firmness of his cheek, to soothe away the worry that tautened his face.

'Don't worry, Mel, darling. I'll look after you,' she whispered faintly.

He laughed softly and kissed the palm of her hand, a soft, warm, comforting kiss. 'Poor darling, you aren't fit to look after yourself, let alone me,' he whispered.

He held another warm drink to her lips and she drank, so glad he was there. She felt herself drifting away again and fought it, afraid that he might be gone when she eventually awoke.

When she opened her eyes again she saw him kneeling across the room with his hand up the chimney, and when she looked again there was a coal fire blazing in the Victorian cast-iron grate. She thought she must be dreaming or hallucinating.

'I'm not very good at this sort of thing,' she heard him murmur a few minutes later, 'but I'm going to try and bath you.'

She lay like a rag doll as he bathed her face and neck with fragrant soft water, his touch smooth and gentle over her burning skin. The sensation was delicious and blissfully she shut her eyes. Her breasts felt so sensitive as he ran his warm, soapy hands over them. She allowed him the intimacy because this was all a dream, really, such a beautiful dream. Mel touching her, comforting her, bathing her with silky warm water. She never wanted it to end, this feeling of safety and security. Water? There wasn't any; the pipes were frozen. Yes, this was a dream.

'There isn't any water,' she croaked.

'Melted snow,' he told her, his voice low so as not to distress her. 'Scented with your perfume. Have you ever had a snow bath before?'

She smiled weakly. 'Never. It's wonderful,' she whispered.

'Try and roll over, then. I'll bathe your back.'

He helped her over and she lay with her face half buried in the pillow. 'Mel, I haven't any clothes on,' she mumbled, realising she was naked but not having the strength to do anything about it.

'I can't bath you with your nightie on, can I? Besides, it was damp with fever.'

'Am I ill?' she croaked.

'You're getting better,' he assured her.

After patting her dry he helped her into a clean cotton nightie—one he must have found in the airing cupboard. It was ancient, but soft and comforting on her skin. He took the patchwork quilt from the bed, wrapped it around her shoulders and carried her over to an armchair by the fire. Out of her dream machine—the bed—she realised this was for real, and reality was suddenly disturbing and confusing.

'Mel, why are you here?' she asked, watching him as he set about changing the sheets on the double bed.

'It doesn't matter for now, Jade,' he said without looking at her. 'I just want to get you better.'

'Is it the flu?'

'Yes, a nasty one too—worse than...' He stopped mid-sentence and, weak in the head as she was, Jade could have finished the sentence for him. Worse than Nadia's.

She turned her pale face to the glowing coals in the grate. What would have happened to her if he hadn't come? It really wasn't a dream. Mel was here and looking after her and being so kind and thoughtful. She shook her muzzy head, trying to recall what had happened so far. Had he called her darling, had he really bathed her fevered skin with melted snow?

'Was...was I delirious?'

'Burning with a terrible fever.' He came and stood over her. 'You're coming out of it, though.'

NATALIE FOX   63

She nodded and tried to smile. 'Thank you, Mel,' she whispered.

He said nothing, didn't even smile, just lifted her from the chair, and she clung to him, leaning her head against his neck and breathing in his scent. It overwhelmed her with memories of the past, when touching him had been a joy that never diminished, when she'd been with him heart and soul, knowing that the future was certain and promised so much happiness. She bit her lip as he lowered her down onto the cool, clean sheets then propped the pillows up behind her. None of that could ever happen again—that feeling of belonging to someone you loved and who loved you in return. He loved someone else now.

'Mel,' she breathed painfully. 'Nadia—'

'Leave it, Jade.'

'I...I can't, Mel. She's your...you should be with her.'

'She's all right,' he assured her quietly. 'Her sister is with her. I'm here. Leave it at that.'

She did. She was too weak to do otherwise. Mel went downstairs to make her a drink and Jade lay back against the fresh pillows and drifted in the apricot glow of the room. She'd lost a day of her life in this bed, thrashing around in a fever, Mel caring for her. She didn't know why he was here and she couldn't begin to imagine. It hurt her head to think too deeply. Now was this room, warmed by a fire, shadowed by the flames from that fire, safe and secure with Mel. It was enough.

It was dark outside, night again, but there was brightness, the moon reflected off the snow. She'd never had a winter with him. She'd loved him in the summer. She loved him now, she realised. She didn't want to love him but she did. And he was here and not with Nadia and she wondered about that. But wondering hurt and made her head swim.

'Could you manage some soup?'

Her stomach recoiled at the thought and she opened her eyes. 'I couldn't, not yet.'

'Drink this, then.' He sat on the edge of the bed, in jeans and a thick dark blue jumper with a cable pattern down the front. He looked so strong and handsome and so deeply concerned for her. His cold fingers brushed hers as he handed her a mug of steaming lemon drink.

'You're cold. You might have this flu bug,' she said with concern. She'd be there for him if he did go down with it, she thought. She'd love him and comfort him and . . .

He smiled. 'I had the jab; besides, a flu bug wouldn't dare.'

She smiled and sipped her drink. 'Am I drinking melted snow?'

'No, bottled water from the fridge and one of those cold-cure powders. I found some sachets in the kitchen drawer. The doctor wouldn't come out because of the terrible weather. The central heating is out because of the frozen pipes. I found coal and lit the fire here and one downstairs. Hopefully the warmth they generate will help the pipes defrost.'

'My, you have been busy,' she teased softly.

He held her eyes, unsmiling, looking more troubled than she had ever seen him before. 'Sleep now, Jade. Talking is exhausting you.'

He took the mug from her fingers, drew the duvet up under her chin and bent and brushed a light kiss across her temples. She fell asleep with the softness of his lips warming her skin.

When she awoke later she was shivering. She felt pressure against her back. Mel was lying on the top of the bed alongside her. He lifted his head when she stirred.

'You're still shivering.'

'Was I before?' she asked.

'A fever again. I tried to warm you.'

'I feel awful, Mel,' she groaned. 'I hate this flu. My body is sore and my bones hurt and I'm so miserable and cold.'

'It's night and the temperature has dropped.'

Jade felt him get up from the bed and she cried out at the loss of his comforting weight from next to her.

'It's all right,' he breathed. She felt him slide under the duvet. 'Here, let me hold you.'

She clung to him, wrapping her arms around him and nestling her head against his warm blue sweater. Mel was here with her, holding her. Her skin was raw and she moaned as his jeans grazed against her thighs.

'You're hurting me,' she groaned. 'Your jeans are so rough.'

He tensed against her and then heaved himself up on one elbow to look down at her pale face. She realised a candle was burning on the table by the bed. No electricity. It was all getting worse. She looked up into his eyes; hers were filled with tears of misery.

His voice was very grave when he spoke. 'Jade, if I take them off we are both in trouble. You understand what I'm saying?'

Suddenly she did. Burning with embarrassment and shame, she went to push him away, but he grasped her wrists and held them. He was tense with anger. 'Jade, it is hard enough just lying on this bed with you fully clothed. If I touch your skin—'

'Don't, Mel,' she pleaded. 'I didn't mean that... I couldn't...I wouldn't.'

Oh, she hadn't meant what he thought, but deep down didn't she long for the contact? Long for how it had once been? Uncomplicated love with none of the doubts and fears of the present that were invading her senses so disastrously?

'I know, I know,' he soothed, lowering his head as if understanding and sorry for being angry with her.

'Don't leave me,' she bleated, and coiled into him.

'I won't,' he breathed against her hair, relaxing down onto the bed and wrapping his arms around her.

She thought she must have slept because she felt different after a while. Still floaty, as if her body didn't belong to her, but warmer. Mel was hard against her, breathing evenly in sleep. One leg was across her, protective and warm and...naked. She remembered his rough jeans and how he wouldn't take them off and how his refusal had filled her with embarrassment. But at some time he *had* taken them off, though he still wore a shirt. It was soft and warm and fragrant against her thin cotton nightie.

She dared to touch him, smoothing her hand down the front of his shirt, just allowing her fingertips to stray between the buttons, to touch his skin and the hair of his chest. He was asleep and wouldn't know.

Her whole body ached for him. She couldn't help herself. Her head was muzzy with longing for him to reach out for her, to gather her into his arms and to hold her for ever and make the future live for her again.

'Don't, Jade—for God's sake don't!' he grated, so thickly that the words came out in a blur.

A sob caught in her throat, a sob of shame and loss and pity for them both, but she was powerless to move away. Too weak, too drowsy to roll away from his magnetism and save her pride from more bruising. She lay motionless apart from the slight heaving of her chest as she tried to control the sobs of anguish in her breast.

And then he moved and slid his arms around her to gather her close to him. He held her gently yet strongly, and she felt the thud of his heart against her own and his mouth pressed in her hair. She lay in the delicious folds of his embrace, her small fists clenched tightly against his shirtfront, trying to control the flood of feeling that rushed through her body as he held her so closely and tenderly.

But it was impossible. She let it wash through her— the desire and the need. She let it speed up her heart beat and spin her senses and didn't think beyond the moment. She tried not to think of the past either because that would remind her of her sad vulnerability now, in wanting a man she couldn't have.

His mouth moved against her hair, then the sensitive area behind her ears, and then suddenly his warm lips were grazing small kisses against her throat. Drowsy, dizzy with longing, she moaned softly, a small, whimpering plea for mercy that went unheeded. His mouth sought hers in the dreamy, floaty world she was entrapped in, this world of unreality where nothing, but nothing mattered but their bodies and hearts responding to a delicious need. She parted her lips for him, to draw him into her very being, to lose herself in his.

In a daze of desire Jade slid her hand up under his shirt, desperate to touch the length of his body after so long. As she slid her hands around his back and drew him to her she felt his arousal hard against her thigh and hope surged like an eternal spring. He still wanted her, as much as she still wanted him. There was no resistance as the kiss deepened dangerously, his tongue insistent and probing the soft inner flesh of her mouth. Nothing could stop the world spinning on its axis as they

clung passionately to each other, their bodies bonding
heatedly.

But then a groan of despair from Mel brought Jade
back to earth with a thud. He tore his mouth from hers
and lifted himself away from her, swearing quietly under
his breath. He rolled away from her and lay on his back,
chest heaving, raking both hands through his hair.

'What the hell do you think you're doing to me, Jade?'
he growled.

In horror Jade turned her face into the pillow and
started to cry softly. What a fool she'd been to let her
heart take over, to allow his gentle seduction to in-
fluence her so deeply. But she was ill. She didn't know
what she was doing and he was blaming *her*. Didn't he
know, didn't he understand that she wasn't in control?

She choked back a sob and bit the pillow. She was
going out of her mind, wanting him, knowing he could
never be hers for longer than it would take for them to
make love. He belonged to Nadia, and yet, yes, she had
wanted him, indeed had nearly taken him, and if she
had she would have died of shame afterwards—for
herself, for him, for the whole wretched world.

'Get...get out of my bed, Mel Biaggio!' she cried
into her damp pillow. But as soon as she had said it she
realised he had already gone. She rolled over. He was
standing naked by the fire, leaning on the mantelpiece
and staring into the hot coals. He was still aroused and
Jade let out a silent moan of desperation. He really
wanted her and she ached for him so badly it was a pain
deep within her. After all this time and all they had been
through they still wanted each other. But his need was
ephemeral, simply a need for a woman—any woman—
if the opportunity arose, she reminded herself with a
cold heart.

She tried to get out of bed and managed at last, weakly steadying herself by grasping the headboard. He heard the movement and turned his head to look at her. His face was drawn.

'Get back into bed, Jade; you're not ready to get up yet.' He came across to her and eased her back down onto the edge of the bed. She stared up at him as he put on his shirt and stepped into his jeans, right in front of her. He wasn't aroused any more.

'You know how close we came just now?' His voice was an accusing growl.

Jade lowered her head and stared at the rug at her bare feet. She nodded, not uttering a word of confirmation.

'You would have hated me after,' he added in that same accusing tone.

Her head shot up defiantly and her eyes were wide and misty. 'Then I wish we had, Mel,' she bit out. 'Because I want to hate you. Nothing would give me greater pleasure than to hate you!'

He went to turn away but Jade grabbed at the sleeve of his sweater. She wasn't going to let him turn his back on her and leave her with all the guilt. 'Don't just turn away and don't try to blame me for what nearly happened. You were in my bed—'

'Not for what you think, though,' he stormed at her, and pulled his sleeve from her grasp. 'You were cold and shivering—'

'And you were warming me, naked!' she argued.

'You kept moaning that your skin was sore and my clothes were rough on you.'

She remembered and hung her head again. 'I'm sorry,' she uttered weakly, the fight slipping from her.

'So am I,' he growled, and left her to go and sit in the chair by the fire, leaning down to forcefully shove a log on top of the coals. The sudden flames lit his grave face and Jade's heart squeezed helplessly.

'Isn't there any electricity?' she asked forlornly. She leaned back against the pillows so that she could watch him, Mel, here with her, angry and yet looking after her, holding her and kissing her and then not allowing it to go further. He was strong, so much stronger than she was, and she resented that. He seemed to have his life completely in control whereas hers was a mess.

'There's a power cut. Three inches of snow and the world goes mad.' His tone was contemptuous.

'You're mad with the world and with me.' She sighed, and her voice was weak with torn emotions and fatigue as she said, 'You never used to be so angry, Mel.'

He smiled without humour, leaned back in the chair and closed his eyes. His face was side-on to her and she could see his eyes were shut, and that even if he opened them she wouldn't be able to read his expression. It helped for what she wanted to ask him.

'Have you been angry all these four years?'

He didn't answer.

'Do you talk to Nadia the way you talk to me—angry and embittered?'

He didn't answer.

'Do you love her more than you loved me?' she asked bravely, wondering where this sudden burst of courage was coming from.

His shoulders stiffened.

She was getting to him. And hurting herself in the process. She didn't really want to know, did she? But she wasn't well and this flu bug was making her do and say things she wouldn't normally.

'My birthday was the worst night of my life, Mel,' she whispered, closing her eyes. 'I didn't know my father was going to do what he did. He's always tried to run people's lives. It's why my mother left. I've known Nicholas all my life, since we were children. We were always together, never lovers, always friends. When I met you I knew what love was. I should have told you about Nicholas but—'

The click of the bedroom door snapped open Jade's eyes. She looked across the room to the fire. It burned brightly but Mel wasn't in the chair beside it. She was alone in the darkened room, along with her incoherent mutterings. A sob of despair caught in her throat and she slid down the bed and closed her eyes tightly to blot it all out.

The room was bright when she awoke. The fire was out but the room was warm. A repetitive click from the radiator in the background was an indication that life was thrumming through the central heating system. Shakily Jade got out of bed and padded to the window, the life seeping gently back into her own bones. Fine rain was falling and there was a constant drip from the roof tiles. The pines in the forest at the end of the garden were already shedding their mantle of snow in the thaw.

The door opened behind her and she turned to see Mel coming into the room with a tray. He was freshly showered, his dark hair damp and slicked, but the growth of beard shocked her.

'You shouldn't be out of bed,' he said, putting the tray down on the bed. 'You must eat today. Get your strength back. I found eggs in the fridge from your last visit—I checked the box and luckily they're not past their sell-by date—and bread in the freezer. Thankfully the electricity wasn't off long enough—'

'Mel,' Jade interrupted, still studying the jet-black growth of hair on his face. It puzzled her. 'What day is it?'

'Monday.'

'Monday!' she wailed. Her hand went to her forehead. She couldn't believe it! 'I . . . I came on Friday night and—'

'You've been very ill, Jade.'

So ill that she had lost days out of her life!

Mel buttered bread for her. She sat on the edge of the bed with him, weak and stunned and trying hard to come to her full senses. So much had happened and it was all still a bit blurred, but the one thing that stood out was Mel's warm kisses and then his terrible withdrawal from her. Had that really happened?

'Have you eaten?' she asked in a murmur as he handed her a warm plate of scrambled eggs and bread and butter. He'd done this for her and . . . and she couldn't bear it, thinking he might care when he didn't really.

'Yes, earlier.'

'You have a beard.'

'I didn't think I'd be staying so long.'

'Why did you come?' There had to be a reason, and it was nothing to do with wanting to be here.

He gave her a rueful smile. 'I told you you couldn't afford country weekends but you wouldn't listen. There's so much to be done, more than you realise. I followed you down and expected to get back the same night or, at the latest, the early hours of the morning.'

Extraordinarily, she was disappointed. Yet she should have guessed what his reason had been. Deep down, she had known. But acceptance was something else. She forked some egg into her mouth; it was good.

'How did you get in?' she asked, her head clearing some more, the food helping.

'The door was open.'

'It couldn't have been,' she protested, but on second thoughts it could have. She hadn't been well when she'd arrived—headachy and cold and not herself at all. 'So you came in and found me.'

'I found the house freezing cold with all the lights on, and when I ventured upstairs you were in bed, moaning. I felt your brow and you were burning with fever. The rest you know.' He got up and, taking his tea to the window, stood drinking it and gazing out at the thawing countryside.

Jade ate what she could, occasionally glancing at him warily. The rest she didn't know, not all of it. He had been here the whole weekend looking after her. What had been going through his mind? Eventually she put down the plate and sipped her tea.

'You needn't have stayed,' she said softly. 'You could have—'

He turned to look at her and the blank expression in his eyes gave her no reason to hope that he had stayed for any reason other than concern for a fellow human being. 'I couldn't leave you. You needed me,' he muttered.

What would he say if she told him she needed him for ever? she wondered. Would he give up Nadia and come back to her?

'I would have thought Nadia needed you too,' she ventured. She watched his face for a change of expression.

'She's on the road to recovery, and besides, as I told you, her sister is with her. You had no one.'

'So you felt sorry for me.' And she was to be pitied, she supposed. She was pathetic.

He smiled then, a genuine one, and came across the room to her. Jade's heart fluttered nervously. He squatted down, took the cup from her fingers and put it down with his on the rug next to him. He held her fingers lightly in his hands and his voice was soft and low as he spoke.

'Yes, I felt sorry for you, and at this moment in time I feel very sorry for myself as well. I know what you're trying to do, Jade; you're trying to draw me out, find out how I really feel about you. You keep mentioning Nadia but she has no place here. You told me a lot of things while you were delirious—tried to explain what happened that night and—'

Jade moaned and dropped her head in embarrassment. 'Please—'

'Please what? Don't embarrass you? I'm not meaning to, Jade. I just don't want you getting too many wrong ideas.'

Her heart contracted painfully. He maybe cared a little, but that was all. He was trying to tell her that none of this mattered, that the only reason he had stayed to nurse her was that she was some poor wretch who had no one else. But he had called her darling and other things, and led her to believe . . .

'Wrong ideas?' she challenged croakily, tears burning her eyes. 'I might have been delirious but I wasn't totally out of my mind, Mel. I felt you. You kissed me—you are always kissing me—exorcising ghosts, you say. You even suggested my total submission just might be the cure-all.' Her eyes were wide with pain and incomprehension. Her voice lowered to a whisper. 'You had your chance, Mel, so why didn't you take it?'

He let go of her fingers, almost thrusting them away from him in disgust. He stood up and went to walk away.

'And you're always doing that, Mel,' she cried, halting him immediately. 'Walking away when it gets too hot for you and you start to hear something that is close to the truth. What is it—a guilty conscience?'

He spun round and faced her angrily. 'You are the one who should have the conscience, Jade. Not me. I don't operate with two lovers—'

'You very nearly did last night, or whatever night it was!' she cried heatedly, getting to her feet to challenge him. 'You nearly—'

'Yes, nearly!' he thrust back at her. 'And it's thanks to me and not you that we didn't go all the way!'

Jade gasped at that, a hand going to her mouth in shame.

'OK, you didn't really know what you were doing—but then again perhaps you did; perhaps, like me, you nearly lost control,' he went on. 'It would have been so damn easy to make love, because we wanted it so badly and couldn't help it. But then what? All it would have amounted to would have been some momentary sexual relief. Climax and then full stop, going nowhere. Because nothing would have changed. I still wouldn't be able to trust you.'

'Trust me!' Jade echoed in a wail of indignation. 'You have never had anything to mistrust me over, only what's in your mind. Nicholas was a part of my life but not the important part that you were. I told you that.'

His eyes narrowed threateningly. 'Yes, this weekend, half out of your mind with delirium. Four years after the event.'

'Oh, no, Mel Biaggio. I'm not taking that,' she cried angrily. 'I tried to tell you then, when you were storming away from my party. You wouldn't listen then and you really didn't hear this time. You wanted to punish me then and you want to punish me now. Bathing me, caring for me, warming me and then the final rejection. You came here and found me ill, saw the opportunity for revenge and snatched at it.'

He stepped towards her and Jade shrank back as he towered over her. He gripped her shoulders, the force of the pressure he was exerting nearly lifting her off the ground.

'The rejection was for self-preservation, Jade, and if you can't recognise that then you haven't learnt much since we parted. Making love to you this once might not have been enough. I might have wanted you again and again, like I did four years ago. I'm not going through that torture again, Jade—never!'

He let her go but didn't move back from her. His body was stiff with tension, his eyes narrowed with anger. He controlled it all, though, and spoke calmly and rationally at last.

'Now that I know you are strong enough to argue with me I'll leave you and get back to London. I've already stayed too long. I'd advise you not to come back to work too soon, because when you do you will need your wits about you.'

Jade stared at him in dismay. How could he be so cold and harsh after being so loving and caring all weekend? Work—how could he think of it after all that had happened during her illness? He had kissed her tenderly and passionately and you couldn't do that if you didn't care. But there was Nadia. He and his Italian honour wouldn't allow Jade Ritchie in his heart any more. What had happened this lost weekend had been a weakness on both their parts. He had been morally strong and was being strong now. She had no choice but to match his strength, and she would. No more weakness where he was concerned.

She took a steadying breath. 'Yes, you'd better get back,' she said resignedly. 'Though what excuse you will give to Nadia I can't imagine.'

'I've already given my excuse,' he told her. 'The phones didn't go down with the weather. We've spoken every night.'

Jade swallowed painfully. Yes, of course he would have phoned his dearly beloved, but she didn't think for a minute he had told her where he was calling from!

'I'll... I'll be in the office tomorrow...'

'No, Jade,' he told her firmly. 'Next week. I'll look after things for you. You're not strong enough yet.'

If she wasn't strong enough why was he leaving her all alone? Because he had to get back to Nadia, that was why. Blindly she turned away and started to gather together her breakfast things. She was strong enough, and as bitter as she was feeling she had to concede that he had done enough already. She might have died here all alone, cold and with frozen pipes and no electricity.

'Thank you for everything, Mel,' she murmured.

He took the tray from her. 'I'll clear up before I go. There is soup and—'

'I know there's soup!' Jade cried, and then bit her lip. She was showing she didn't want him to leave, which was crazy because she did want him to go, right out of her life, and never to come back again. She lowered her voice. 'I don't feel like eating yet awhile. You're right— you must get back. I've kept you from your life long enough.'

He went out of the room in silence and came back ten minutes later to say goodbye. Jade was back in bed with the duvet pulled up under her trembling chin. He bent and kissed her forehead but it was a condescending kiss, a duty kiss.

'You're cool now. Rest and get plenty of fluids and try to eat something later. I'll call you tonight.'

Jade didn't say a word. She was too choked up inside to speak. She heard him close the front door after him and his car engine starting and the swish of tyres on the drive. Then an awful silence that stretched into eternity.

to speak. She heard him close the front door afterwards

CHAPTER FIVE

IT TOOK Jade only a fleeting second to take in the impact of Nadia's presence in the art department. There had always been a buzz in the offices when the guys were firing on all cylinders. Today there was a mega-buzz as Jade pushed open the swing doors and stepped into the studio. There was a group gathered around Dave Rand's drawing board and Jade sensed that Nadia would be the nucleus.

Her first day back and she had to face this. It was enough to give her a relapse. Jade shrugged off her coat and draped it over her arm. She hadn't been to her own office yet; the buzz of creativity had drawn her straight up to the studio.

On her entrance Dave Rand, the more senior of her artists, turned, and the group around his desk parted like the Red Sea to reveal a very beautiful Nadia.

Jade hadn't doubted she would be beautiful, but in fact she was exquisite: dark, with gamine features framed by a mass of tumbling chestnut hair that almost reached to her waist. She wore skin-tight black trousers and a sloppy black sweater that skimmed the cheeks of her perfect bottom. Her jewellery—droopy earrings, beads and bangles—was ethnic, profuse and noisy, her perfume Eastern and exotic.

She was arty and charismatic and radiated flair and style, and Jade felt wave after wave of unaccustomed jealousy wash over her. To add insult to injury Jade noted that she was as petite as herself. They said men were attracted to the same sort of woman. Mel obviously went for tiny women he could *try* to dominate.

'Jade...' Dave was the first to speak, frowning with concern. 'Good to see you back, but rushing it a bit, aren't you? Mel said you wouldn't be in till next week.'

'I'm fine,' Jade told him. Mel had called last night and she hadn't told him she intended driving up the next morning. She did feel fine, sort of. It had been unbearable staying on at the house after he had left and she had determined to get back to normal as soon as possible.

'You might look fine but you can't be,' came from behind her, and Jade swung around to face Mel. He didn't look at all pleased to see her, but then she hadn't really expected him to be now that Nadia was here with him. Jealousy burst that ridiculous little bubble of hope that had persisted on and off till now. 'I told you not to come in till next week.'

The group dispersed, except for Nadia.

'You don't tell me what to do in my own company, Mel,' she told him calmly. 'And you don't reprimand me in front of my staff.' Her eyes were unflinching as she faced him. This was the only way—to harden her heart against more hurt.

Mel's eyes narrowed. 'And you don't reprimand *me* for reprimanding you in front of your staff either,' he said tightly, meaning Nadia.

For Nadia's sake Jade kept her retort tightly buttoned; the girl had shifted uncomfortably at the crossfire between them.

Mel introduced them and as Jade shook Nadia's hand in greeting she was surprised to feel a tremor in the girl's grasp. She wondered if her own had given anything away.

'Pleased to meet you, Jade.' Nadia smiled hesitantly. 'I do hope you're feeling better. It's a lousy bug and I wouldn't wish it on my worst enemy.'

Heavens, was Jade her worst enemy? Her throat tightened at the thought of how this girl must be feeling, working with Mel's one-time lover...*if* she knew. Had Mel told her?

'I hope you are feeling better too,' Jade returned politely, not at all sure how to take her or her own feelings at the moment. Here she was, face to face with the woman who was going to marry Mel and unable to determine how she felt. Initially she'd been jealous but the wobbly handshake had confused Jade. It gave the stunning girl a vulnerability she hadn't expected.

Nadia laughed, a soft, almost nervous tinkle of mirth that no doubt would win the hearts of all the men in the art department, if it hadn't already. 'I think with the depth of caring we both received a good recovery was inevitable,' Nadia said, her eyes bright as she looked up at Mel with obvious adoration and gratitude.

Jade felt herself go cold all over, as if her life's blood had drained down to her ankles. Nadia knew Mel had nursed her too? When Mel had told her he had made his excuses to Nadia over the phone she hadn't thought he might have told her the truth—that he was nursing her back to health. With an aching heart she wondered if he had bathed Nadia as well, snuggled up to her to keep her warm... Oh, no, I can't bear this, she thought in misery. It's worse than revenge; it's going to be a slow death by emotional torture.

'H-how are you settling in?' Jade forced herself to ask.

She didn't even know when Nadia had started. It was Thursday, and though Mel had phoned every night since leaving on Monday he hadn't mentioned Nadia.

'Everyone has been so wonderful. I feel as if I've been here for years already.' She smiled but Jade thought she detected just a trace of uncertainty in her eyes. 'Thank you for giving me this opportunity, Jade; it's—'

'We must leave you to get on, Nadia,' Mel interrupted quickly—so quickly that it aroused Jade's curiosity. Did he think Nadia was getting too familiar too soon? 'Go through those artwork details with Dave,' he added efficiently.

Curiosity piled on curiosity as he took Jade's elbow and guided her away from Nadia and an eagerly approaching Dave, who looked besotted already with the dazzling little newcomer.

'When did she start?' Jade asked as they went through the swing doors to the stairs.

'Yesterday,' Mel told her. 'I must say your staff have made her most welcome. She'll be OK.'

Before they stepped into her office Jade turned to him. 'What do you mean she'll be OK? Any reason why she shouldn't be? I thought she was an award-winner. This company must be a bit of a let-down to her after—'

Mel interjected with an impatient sigh. 'Jade, don't put your own company down. How can you expect to pull yourself out of all this if you don't think positively?'

He was right, of course, as always. She turned into her office without another word, thinking that Mel had very successfully evaded what she'd asked concerning Nadia. In due course she would no doubt find out why he had placed her here, because for sure there must be a reason. It was a thought which had suddenly blossomed now that Nadia had actually started with the company. She was a successful freelance commercial artist and engaged to Mel and really had no need to work other than for pleasure. And just now she had thanked Jade for giving her an opportunity. An opportunity for what?

'Oh,' Jade breathed, flinging her coat down on a chair by the door. 'Mel, what's this?' He'd followed her in and she grazed her high heels on the carpet as she swung to face him, frowning disconcertedly.

'Another desk, as you can see.'

She watched him as he crossed to the coffee-machine, as if he belonged in the room. For some reason Jade felt a frisson of unease.

'Yes, I can see it's a desk and I can see the telephone on it and a lot of paper and office paraphernalia, none of which is mine. What exactly do you think you are doing?'

He looked her directly in the eye as if he had absolutely nothing to hide from her and Jade immediately thought he must have.

'I'm doing my job, Jade.'

'Troubleshooters don't move in and take complete control, Mel,' she protested, the frisson of unease swelling into something more scary. She felt as if she was being taken over here, her authority usurped! She'd asked for help but wasn't he taking it a bit too far?

'They do if it is needed,' he said coolly. He finished pouring two coffees. He brought hers over and put it down on her desk and without looking at her crossed to his to pick up the phone.

In two strides a worried Jade was across the room and snatching the phone from his hand. She thrust it down on the desk. 'It is *not* needed, Mel,' she insisted, her dark eyes flashing with determination. 'You are going above and beyond your profession. I asked for help and advice on a consultancy basis. I didn't ask for your permanent presence here in my office and I didn't ask for your mistress taking over my art department either. Next you'll be moving in your cousins and your household pets!'

He smiled, not even taking her seriously. 'I don't have any household pets.'

'Mel, I'm serious!' Jade cried. 'What exactly do you think you're doing?'

His eyes darkened suddenly. 'Exactly what you are paying me to do,' he almost shouted. 'Trying to save your company from the trash bin, and from what I've seen here since getting involved I'll be hard-pressed to recycle a paper clip at the end of it!'

Stunned, Jade gaped at him, her heart racing. Was he serious? Was all this serious—this necessity to oversee every move she made? Was it all worse than she had imagined? What did he know that she didn't?

She swallowed nervously. 'What's happening?'

'You have a week to spare for me to read the list of problems out to you?' he drawled sarcastically.

White-lipped, Jade stepped backwards and slumped into her seat. Her father would never forgive her for this. He had trusted her and had enough confidence in her abilities to let her take over. And she had let him down.

Mel came across to her and sat on the edge of her desk. 'I'm sorry, that was out of order,' he said quietly.

She nodded, accepting his apology, though she thought it could have come with more feeling.

'So tell me something,' he began. 'What was going on in that pretty little head of yours last year when your top artist left with his greedy little fists clutching your best contracts? You could have stopped it, you know. A few well-timed phone calls to those clients and you could have smoothed everything out for yourself.'

Jade lifted her chin and glared at him. She knew why she had missed what was going on and if she told him he'd probably laugh in her face. The whole awful business had coincided with Nicholas's and Trisha's engagement announcement and sent her spiralling down into a pit of depression and self-pity. She didn't begrudge them their happiness one iota but oh, how it had brought home to her her own empty life. It had been one of her worst times, missing Mel so, knowing that she had lost the only love of her life. Was it any wonder she hadn't been thinking straight at the time?

'It was just one of those things,' she admitted with a shrug, looking away from him. 'For some reason I wasn't as sharp as I usually am.' It was a feeble attempt to account for her actions but all she could come up with without making a complete fool of herself.

'A lover maybe?' Mel suggested with a measure of malice that didn't go unnoticed by Jade.

It was an appalling suggestion and she narrowed her eyes at him. 'No lover, Mel. I learnt my lesson with you. You spoke of not trusting me a few days ago—well, the same goes for me too. I wouldn't trust another man with what's left of my emotions since you wrung the life out of them.'

'So you lead a celibate life, do you?' he mocked.

'I would say that was obvious as I don't have a lover,' she retorted, very much resenting the way this conversation was going. 'Anyway, I object to the suggestion that I would allow a lover to interfere with the way I run the company. It makes me sound as if hormones run my life.'

'Trouble is, women in commerce sometimes do allow hormones to interfere in their business decisions.'

'That is a blatantly sexist remark, Mel, and you are only saying it for effect,' she said with contempt.

'Yes, very probably,' he conceded unexpectedly, effectively getting out of that one.

'Are you serious about moving into this office with me?' she asked. She didn't think she'd be able to bear it if he was. There were moments when she truly despised him and others when she felt utterly vulnerable in his presence, and the combination of the two was wearing her ragged.

He didn't answer straight away. He held her dark eyes for an uncomfortably long moment. He seemed to be trying to read her thoughts. Jade gave nothing away. This week she had resolved to keep her emotions under wraps and she was doing her best to keep that resolve. Eventually he broke the eye contact and got up from her desk and went to his own.

'It will only be on a part-time basis,' he told her, drinking his coffee and flicking through his personal organiser. He lifted the phone again and dialled a number but carried on talking to her. 'I have other commitments but I need to keep close to what is going on here.'

He wanted to keep close to Nadia, that was all, she conceded dismally. Why had she allowed it all to happen? He was here and had wasted no time at all in slipping Nadia in. She might have talent and bring valuable new clients to the company but she was also his mistress.

She wished with all her heart that she hadn't listened to Nicholas because now she was in too deep to get out. As far as the company was concerned she had to admit there was a new vibrancy about the place. She had only been off sick a handful of days and in that time Mel had turned it all around. And turned her emotions inside out and on end.

'I must admit he's working a miracle, Nicholas. This Nadia talent is pulling in some fantastic work.'

Jade was dishing up a lasagne she had been laboriously preparing since getting in from work. They didn't often dine together but Trisha was up north on an investment course and Nicholas was at a loose end, and as they had hardly seen each other lately an evening in together was an ideal opportunity to catch up with each other's gossip.

'The builders are in converting the ground floor,' Jade went on. 'He's organised it all—banks, leasing equipment, everything. He spends quite a bit of time in the office and it's all paying off.' Jade pushed a plate across to him as he poured the wine.

'And exactly how much are you paying him for this miracle he's working?' Nicholas asked.

Jade looked at him across the table, thinking that no two men could be so different. They were both good-looking but in such different ways. Mel was dark, swarthy, sophisticated, the sort of man who could fit several roles in life—pirate, bank robber, the financial troubleshooter that he was. Nicholas, with his mid-brown hair, steady hazel eyes, slim, straight, upright figure, exuding stability, could only ever be what he was—a stockbroker.

'Did you hear me, Jade?'

'Yes—yes, I heard,' Jade replied absently. Mel was always in her thoughts, always. She wished it weren't that way but it was. She was fighting it, but at vulnerable times, such as when she was tired, she seemed incapable of stopping herself from sliding into that pit of remembrance and thinking of all they had once been to each other. 'I don't know what his fee is yet,' she went on. 'He said he'd name his price when it was all over.'

Nicholas's fork stayed suspended in mid-air. 'I hope you're not serious, Jade. You should have fixed a fee before you went into this,' he remonstrated.

Jade shrugged and got on with her food. Yes, she knew she should have done, but what Nicholas didn't know was that she knew Mel and she trusted him—where business was concerned, that was.

'It sounds as if he's got his feet well under the table,' Nicholas went on. Jade looked up to see him frowning. It made her ill at ease straight away.

'What's wrong, Nicholas? You recommended him.'

'Only on the strength of him sorting out a friend's problems, the friend in question having a staff of four hundred, not sixteen as in your case,' he said pointedly.

'Stop messing around, Nicholas. Get to what is bothering you.'

Nicholas lifted his wineglass to his lips before speaking. Jade watched him curiously and waited.

'Mel Biaggio took only five days to put him on the straight and narrow and he didn't need to move into the boardroom permanently to do it.'

'I really don't get your point.' Jade shrugged but she couldn't get rid of the unease inside her. She'd often thought Mel was going over the top in the hours he put into her small ad agency, and now Nicholas thought it odd.

Nicholas suddenly grinned. 'I think he fancies you.'

'Don't be absurd!' Jade protested quickly, probably too quickly. She took a great gulp of wine. She couldn't tell Nicholas the truth—that once they had been lovers and because of him they weren't any more. Mel hated her now—well, maybe not exactly hated—hate was such a strong word—but certainly he didn't care for her any more. He was doing a job of work, not hanging around because he fancied her.

'I don't think it's unreasonable to suggest the man could be besotted with you. You're beautiful and he hasn't exactly got the reputation of a Benedictine monk. Watch out, Jade; he might be after your heart.'

'And supposing he is and supposing I give it?' she retorted teasingly.

Nicholas shrugged. 'I suppose he'll let you down. Men like him do. Womanisers make deplorable husbands—if they ever get to the altar, that is.'

'Leopards can't change their spots, you mean?'

She really didn't know why she was carrying on this line of conversation. She knew something that Nicholas didn't—that Mel hadn't always been a womaniser. She would stake her life that he had been faithful to her while they were having an affair. Mel had changed his spots for a while and now, apparently, he had changed them back again. Because of his commitment to Nadia he had held back from her at Bankton House. She supposed he was quite an honourable man now.

'Exactly,' Nicholas confirmed, helping himself to more lasagne. 'You don't get a reputation like his for nothing.'

'Well, for your information, Mr Reputationless Fields, Mel Biaggio is engaged to be married.'

Why Jade felt the need to leap to his defence she didn't know but here she was doing it, and to Nicholas, who didn't even know him personally and never would.

'That's a surprise,' Nicholas uttered, evidently losing interest.

Jade leaned across the table to him. 'To Nadia, the talent, the lady I was telling you about. The one Mel has put into my art department.'

Suddenly Nicholas was interested again—amazed in fact.

'You have to be joking!' he exclaimed.

'Why should I joke? She's very beautiful and—'

'I'm sure she must be but...well...it's odd. He's successful and you wouldn't think he'd...well...allow his fiancée to... I mean, I'm not putting your company down but it's—'

'I know,' Jade breathed despondently, wishing she'd never brought any of this up. 'I know exactly what you are trying to say and I have to go along with you. It's not as if they need the money...' Her voice trailed off with the sudden realisation that Nadia's salary had never been discussed. Jade shrugged. 'Anyway it's none of our business and—'

'I think you should make it your business, Jade,' Nicholas suddenly cautioned, quite seriously, too. 'If he's engaged to be married he can't be hanging around for you, and he *is* hanging around, Jade. Giving your company far more attention than he should be. You say you haven't fixed a fee for his work. I'd advise you to do that immediately and I'd keep a careful eye on what exactly he and his talent are doing within your company. I'd nail my desk to the floor if I were you.'

Jade didn't need to ask him to spell all that out to her. She knew exactly what he was getting at. At the end of the day Mel Biaggio might name a price she couldn't afford—like control of the company, lock, stock and barrel.

Suddenly she had no appetite for food any more. Jade leaned back in her chair and lifted her wine to her pale lips. Mel wasn't to be trusted after all, not with hearts or companies.

'Don't be silly, Mel. Nadia must have a salary. She isn't your responsibility, she's mine.'

Mel stood up, all potent masculinity, and went to the window, kneading his brow. Jade watched him, uncertain as to his mood. She was still having trouble coping with him being here so much—in her territory, her sexual awareness of him nagging at her silly bones.

Even like this, detached and brooding, he had a magnetism that defied credibility. He'd been like this for days now—unsettled, snappy with her, never with Nadia. Nadia was handled with kid gloves, Jade handled with rubber gloves, as if she was well able to bounce back, which Jade supposed was the impression she gave.

Nadia was turning out to be a strange one. No one could fault her work and the boys in the studio got on well with her but there was a vulnerability about her that flummoxed Jade. Her own feelings about Nadia flummoxed her too. Against her will she found herself liking her and that was definitely puzzling. She had every reason to dislike her intensely; she was the woman who held Mel's heart in her talented little fingers, after all.

Yes, it was all very peculiar. Nadia had flair and originality but she needed reassurance and a lot of TLC. Mel was certainly giving her a lot of tender loving care but not the sort Jade would have thought you gave the woman you were deeply in love with. At times he seemed to treat her as if... Jade couldn't fathom it out really; the only thing she could compare it to was...well...say, doctor and patient—and since when had Mel gained any medical qualifications?

'Mel, did you hear me? I have to instruct Karen, who deals with salaries—'

'I'll deal with it!' Mel suddenly snapped.

'And don't snap at me!' Jade retorted, purposely keeping her own voice calm. 'Remember I still run this company and—'

'I know, I know,' he quickly responded. He slumped down into his chair and looked across at her. 'Sorry, but—'

'I know, I know,' Jade mimicked, waving a hand in the air. 'Pressure of work, Nadia's sensitivity, testosterone!'

He smiled, albeit reluctantly. 'Yes, men have hormones too. That should make you happy.'

Him smiling, reluctantly or otherwise, lifted her spirits. She'd never seen him so tense as he had been lately. She'd questioned it several times, worried for the company and worried for him that because of the past he wouldn't be able to bring himself to tell her if it all turned out to be hopeless. But he was always quick to assure her that everything was going very well, and really she knew that anyway. Three new contracts this week had assured a healthy working environment for many months to come.

'Come downstairs with me,' he suggested, leaping to his feet with a sudden burst of enthusiasm. 'The builders are out to lunch and we can have a snoop around the new studio without some bolshie foreman breathing down our necks.'

Jade got up, not arguing. She hadn't done much of that lately, although perhaps she should have. She was still desperately worried that Mel might indeed have some plan to take over control of the company, but time and time again she asked herself why a man in his professional position should be interested in taking control of a very small ad agency. Which was stupid, she reprimanded herself now, because there was a host of reasons why: revenge on her, something for Nadia to dabble in once she and the mighty Mel were wed, a bargaining tool for something bigger.

'By the time you finish with the company, Mel, we'll be a force to reckon with,' she said, fishing for something, although exactly what she wasn't sure.

'I don't like to see talent go to waste,' he told her, holding the door open for her.

Jade wrinkled her nose against dust motes still heavy in the air after the plasterers had finished that morning. The new studio was empty because, as Mel had said, the builders were out at lunch.

'My talent or Nadia's?' she ventured as Mel wandered around the huge open space, inspecting the power points as if he knew what he was doing. Perhaps he did.

'Everyone's,' he said vaguely. 'You'll have a nice little set-up when I've finished.'

'Does Nadia know about you and me, Mel?' she asked.

She'd intended grabbing his full attention and she succeeded. He shot her a black look across the bright but dusty room.

'That we were lovers?' He gave her no space to answer. 'Of course not, and under the circumstances I don't want you telling her either.'

'What circumstances are those?' Jade cleared a space on the wide window-sill with a piece of old cloth and leaned back against it, extending her legs out in front of her.

'She works for you.'

That was a matter of opinion Jade wasn't willing to thrash out at the moment. 'So?'

'So forget it, Jade,' he said wearily.

'How can I forget it? I might let something slip one day.' She hadn't meant it as a threat but from the way he shot a poisoned look at her you'd have thought she'd made a million-dollar blackmail demand.

'If you know what's good for you you'll keep our past well and truly the past and forget it,' he shot at her.

She wished that she could. Wished that she weren't faced with her past every wretched day of her life, in the form of him. Sometimes a certain way he looked at her, eyes soft, crinkled at the corners with humour, brought it all rushing back, so many happy memories, and then the present would hit her and leave her bereft, aching with her loss.

'I find her strange,' Jade admitted, fishing again.

He was back to his wanderings, running a hand over the wooden panelling on one wall. 'You're the only one that does, Jade. She's extremely popular and has settled in well.'

'Considering what?'

He looked at her again, frowning broodily. 'What do you mean, "Considering what?"'

She shrugged. 'I thought it needed adding to your sentence. It was sort of incomplete without it.'

'What the hell are you after, Jade?'

She sighed inwardly. 'The truth, I suppose. I just find it odd that you're here far more than you should be. That Nadia, the love of your life, is working in my studio, not knowing about our past and being a bit odd, sometimes brimming over with confidence and then suddenly going flat—'

'She hasn't been well,' Mel interrupted impatiently.

'Nor have I,' Jade returned. Actually she could partly sympathise with Nadia's mood swings. Since the flu bout she hadn't really felt right herself. Perhaps both of them had come back to work too soon.

'When are you getting married?' She couldn't have asked this sooner—her emotions had been too raw. Actually they still were, but with these emotions had come a new strength lately—or maybe she was just getting harder and more cynical, sharing her office with him and his cold hostility.

'No date fixed,' he muttered.

'When are you going to buy her a ring?' Jade had noticed that Nadia didn't wear a ring on her engagement finger; she did on every one but the third on the left. Maybe it was the Italian way to wear it on another finger.

'A ring isn't compulsory for an engagement.'

Jade's heart began to beat at a different tempo. This didn't sound at all right.

'She sounds a very special lady, then. Most women would see a ring as a very romantic commitment—a binding one too.'

Mel came across the room. He stopped in front of her and leaned towards her, supporting himself with one hand on the panelling around the window. His eyes were dark and accusing.

'Remember our commitment to each other?' he taunted. 'I thought you were a very special lady too, a very special lover. We talked of love, not expensive rings. Was that my mistake? If you'd had an egg-sized diamond glittering on your finger would you have acted any differently?'

Pulsing with the hurt of that, Jade hadn't the strength to fight back with a protest. This was what she got for prying—knife-edged suggestions meant to cut through to the bone of her emotions.

'Personally I don't think so,' he blazed on. 'A material commitment wouldn't have made any difference to what you did to me. I think you did it for kicks.'

'And what you are doing now is returning those kicks, Mel,' she said through thin lips, her throat so dry she could scarcely get the words out. 'I...I might have known you would turn all this around so you could indulge in your weird accusations once more. All I asked was why Nadia didn't wear your ring.'

'*That* is between Nadia and myself,' he emphasised heavily.

Jade shrugged. 'OK. I'm not that curious.' Her eyes sparkled suddenly and she smiled over-sweetly. 'It's girl talk anyway. I'll ask her myself next time we're powdering our noses together.' She went to get up and push past him but he thrust her back down on the window-sill, towering over her. His eyes were glittering darkly and she knew she had irritated him intensely, which had been exactly her intention.

'You'll do nothing of the sort,' he warned roughly. 'Nadia is a very private person. Stick to business and you'll be all right. Get personal with her and you will wish you hadn't.'

His threat found its way into her heart and her curiosity. There was definitely something strange about Nadia. She had a past and Mel didn't want anyone knowing about it. She didn't wear his ring so maybe . . . maybe she was already married.

It could explain a lot of things, like why she was here working in an obscure ad agency when she was the talent she was. Was she in hiding from an irate husband? Was Mel a wife-snatcher? Mel wouldn't get himself involved with a married woman, would he? But she didn't know him any more. He had changed so drastically he could still shock her with something new every day.

'She sounds formidable,' Jade drawled. He didn't frighten her and nor did Nadia. 'Is that why you've never told her about us—scared for your own skin?' she goaded.

He snatched at her wrist and hauled her to her feet. She teetered in front of him, stabilised only by his fierce grip on her.

'No woman is capable of scaring me, Jade. But you— you had the ability to rock my life once. I've tried to forget you and might have succeeded if your cry for help hadn't drawn me back into your life again. Now, in spite of Nadia, I find myself reliving every crippling moment of our affair. You, and what we had that you ruined, isn't what I choose for fireside conversation when I'm with Nadia. I'm warning you, I don't want our past brought up with Nadia. My bloody pride can't take it.'

His grip on her loosened, but just as she thought he was going to turn away from her he changed his mind and gripped her shoulders fiercely. His voice was gravelly when he spoke. 'I wish to hell you had married Nicholas Fields, because then you would be out of my reach. Married, you would be out of temptation's way. This has been the worst business decision of my life.'

His lips on hers were, as ever, the cruellest punishment, the most painful of reminders, the most exquisite pressure. His arms enfolded her slight frame and drew her against his towering strength and she yielded helplessly, her head swimming with the words he had just said and what they meant. She was a temptation to him; he was still trying to get over her and now...now his kissing her meant he was crumbling, wanting her and not able to hold back.

The kiss deepened, all temptation, all desire encapsulated within it. His hands moved around her back, drawing her ever more powerfully into his heady world of passion. One hand smoothed over her breast in a sensual, bone-melting rhythm that set her nerve-endings tingling. Where was her conscience when she needed it? When he kissed her like this, touched her like this, she couldn't think of anyone but themselves. Jade and Mel as it used to be, as it should be. But it wasn't Jade and Mel, it was Nadia and Mel...

She staggered back, blinking rapidly, not sure if she had pulled away or if he had pushed her. She gave him a look of total despair as she read the desire in his glittering eyes. Yes, desire—so damned obvious, so damned cruel. Not love, not regret for the past, nothing but damned animal desire, and ... and she had nearly succumbed and he knew.

With shame flaring in her cheeks, Jade turned away and left him standing alone with a very knowing look darkening his eyes.

CHAPTER SIX

'WHERE are you going?' Mel asked, stepping into the office a short time later. He came and stood by her desk, his dark, hooded eyes resting on her challengingly.

'To see a client,' Jade clipped, buttoning her suit jacket and adjusting the scarf at her throat. She had to get out, away from him and the thoughts of that wretched kiss downstairs.

'Are you sure you're not copping out, unable to face what happened just now?' Infuriatingly, his voice was as smooth as silk.

'What exactly did just happen, Mel?' she asked without looking at him. She scoured her desk drawer for a presentation she had prepared last week and added stoically, before he had a chance to speak, 'We both showed a bit of weakness just now, that's all. I'm sure we can both live with it.'

'Yes, well, a guilty conscience never was one of your strong points.'

'And obviously not one of yours either. A kiss is just as big a betrayal as the whole thing, you know. Don't go all pious on me just because you were the one who copped out last time we nearly made love.'

'You were delirious.'

She looked up at him. He was leaning casually on his desk with his arms folded across his chest, a stance that screamed out that he was winding her up. She smiled sweetly at him. 'So I was. Fancy you recognising it. But then I suppose the women you have associated with over the years have all had degrees in delirium!'

'So you've been charting my amorous progress these last years.' He smiled knowingly.

'Hard not to when every week you give the tabloids reason for featuring you and your libido in their columns.'

'I don't like dining alone.'

'You don't like *sleeping* alone!'

'The papers exaggerate—'

'Huh, there's no smoke without fire!' Her eyes went down to the desk again. Where was that presentation?

'Down to waving that old cliché at me now, are you? Can't you come up with something more original?'

She glared at him then. 'Sadly, no, Mel, because you are so steeped in rigid thinking you wouldn't recognise original if it swung from your armpits.'

'Meaning?'

She took a deep breath. 'Meaning four years ago you believed I had a lover while I was loving you. You refused to listen to my explanations and if you had listened you would have refused to believe that a man and woman can have a relationship built on friendship and not on sex. That's what I mean about rigid thinking.' She stopped and let out a great sigh of impatience. 'I don't know why I'm bothering. I'm wrong, anyway. You aren't steeped in rigid thinking, you bend the rules to suit yourself—'

'You're rambling, Jade,' he interjected, impatient himself now. 'Get to the point you're trying to make.'

She slumped down into her chair and looked at him bleakly. This was ridiculous; they should never have allowed this hurtful conversation to get this far. 'There isn't one. You started all this, kissing me downstairs then cross-examining me about it—'

'It was hardly a cross-examination. Your voluntary input into this conversation has been greater than mine,

Jade. Makes me feel you want to shed your conscience,'
he mocked.

'I haven't one, remember?' she breathed sarcastically.
'Ah, here it is.' She waved the presentation at him. 'My
passport to freedom for the afternoon.' She stood up.

'You can't go out this afternoon; we have work to go
through together,' he protested.

'You're doing such a heroic job here yourself, Mel,
you don't need me. I doubt you and Nadia will notice
I'm not here. But I'll be back.' She swept out of the
office before he could throw another protest in her path,
and though she'd had the last word she didn't feel as if
she had.

Jade read Nicholas's note when she got home. He'd be
away for a few days and Trisha would be dropping in
with the suits he'd asked her to pick up from the cleaners.

Jade screwed up the note and tossed it into the bin.
She wished Nicholas would hurry up and marry Trisha
and move out altogether. Trisha still lived with her
parents so their free time was usually spent in the
apartment and Jade was consequently witness to all their
little domesticities, which made her feel the loss of Mel
ever more poignantly.

She put the coffee-pot on and kicked off her shoes.
It was funny how Trisha totally accepted that there was
nothing but friendship between her and Nicholas. Mel
wouldn't be so understanding if he knew Nicholas stayed
here when he was in town. His Italian-influenced thinking
was too rigid. Men and women couldn't be friends in
his tight world; it was lovers or nothing.

After a long, lazy soak in the bath Jade eyed the
abysmal contents of the fridge. There wasn't much to
excite the palate. As she was contemplating going out
for a take-away something or other the security buzzer

went. She sighed and pressed the button, praying it wasn't Trisha at a loose end without Nicholas and wanting to talk wedding talk. It always made Jade feel more lonely than ever.

'Jade? It's me.'

'Mel!' she croaked into the intercom, instinctively pulling her wrapover sarong-style skirt across her knees, which was ridiculous because he couldn't see her.

'I expected you back this afternoon, Jade,' he said sourly. 'You lose Brownie points for that.'

'Not funny, Mel, not original either. What do you want?'

She glanced at the digital clock on the microwave. He must have come straight from work. If so he'd have Nadia with him. They always went off together when Mel was in the office, and when he wasn't he usually picked her up after work.

'I want to come in. I'm not standing down here for my health,' he snapped back.

Must be the happy hour, Jade mused as she buzzed him in, not looking forward to his biting repartee one iota. She put the coffee-pot on again and went to the door, glancing into the gilt-framed mirror beside it. At least she was dressed, in a long skirt and loose, flowing shirt. Normally she fell into a worn towelling robe after a bath. Tonight she must have had a premonition of some approaching catastrophe, like an earthquake, the end of the world, or a visit from Mel Biaggio!

'I', he had said, so he was alone, which was a minor relief. She opened the door to him and stood back, surprised at the armful of packages he was holding. 'What's all this?'

'Take-away and wine and a briefcase full of work to go through, and before you protest I'm leaving for Paris in the morning and won't be back till next week, so if you want this lot sorted you'll have to put up with my company for a few hours.'

He followed her through and dumped the packages on the breakfast bar.

She looked at him and shrugged. 'You won't get an argument out of me. I've nothing in the fridge, not even the dregs of a wine box, and I wouldn't want you to put off your trip to fairyland for my benefit. Paris, eh? Planning your honeymoon?'

He ignored her sarcasm and clipped open his briefcase. He hadn't even looked around the open-plan area of the apartment. It was decorated in warm terracotta shades, with splashes of blue in the cushions and upholstery and ceramic pots filled with ferns and greenery to give it a Mediterranean feel. He wasn't interested in her life. She sighed and sorted out the cartons. She shouldn't think the way she did, hoping for droplets of warmth and appreciation to fall when she knew it was all hopeless.

'Where's Nadia?'

'Out this evening.'

'Nice for her,' Jade murmured. 'Is this from the Thai restaurant round the corner?'

He looked up. 'Yes, why? No good?'

'It looks and smells wonderful. I've never tried them. I will in future.'

Their eyes met across the breakfast bar and both looked away. Jade wondered if he was thinking along the same lines as herself. They'd used to practically live on take-aways when they were together, too wrapped up in each other to bother wasting time cooking for themselves.

'Where do you want to eat?' she asked. 'At the table or on your lap?'

For the first time he looked around the open-plan area of the apartment. 'This is nice. Light and airy. Totally out of keeping with the Regency façade of the building, though.'

What had she expected—a glowing testimonial to her good taste? She clattered around in the cupboards for plates and glasses. 'Not guilty, I'm afraid. It was like this when I bought it. I just added a few bits of my own. An interior designer lived here before.'

'Not a sympathetic one,' he uttered under his breath as he sorted papers from his briefcase.

He *was* steeped in rigid thinking. No room for change, for compromise, wanting everything just as it should be. He had a point, though, she conceded, gazing around the spacious area, seeing it from his viewpoint. It did seem a shame to modernise an old apartment and drag it screaming into the twentieth century. Perhaps if the agency was doing well by the time Mel had finished with it she'd bring it back to something more traditional. *If* she had any will left.

'Do you still have the apartment at Regent's Park?' she asked, aware that she was making small talk. Since he hadn't answered her question about where he'd like to eat, she set the table and put the foil dishes of Thai food on a table mat in the centre so they could help themselves. She had loved his sumptuous apartment with its high ceilings, cornices and wide doorways. It had been elegant and had reflected his character but somehow she couldn't visualise the arty Nadia flitting round in it with her jewels jangling.

'I took the lease on the whole property,' he told her. 'Planning for the future.'

Planning a family life with Nadia. The thought churned horribly inside her. She might have been a part of that future if... if Mel Biaggio hadn't been so single-minded, old-fashioned, out of order and, well, just Mel Biaggio.

'Nice,' she murmured.

'I remember *nice*,' he said reflectively as he settled the papers between them on the table. 'You always used to mutter it when you were bored or uninterested.'

She couldn't ever remember a time when she'd been bored and uninterested with him. Perhaps all her memories were rose-tinted, not how it had been at all. It was an interesting thought. 'I still do,' she told him lightly. 'Your future with Nadia doesn't interest me, Mel.' It hurt, though, she omitted to say.

'Funny, I don't recall mentioning Nadia.'

Jade sat down at the table and started wrestling with the wine bottle. 'Nadia is your future, isn't she?'

'Possibly. Here, let me open that.'

Jade impatiently thrust the bottle across the table at him. 'I remember *possibly* too; it was usually followed by something banal to change the subject. What's wrong? Do you and Nadia have a problem with your future that you don't want to talk about?'

He poured them each a glass of wine. '*Possibly* you'd be the last person in the world I'd discuss my personal life with,' he said cuttingly.

It didn't put Jade off. 'You didn't say discuss your *problems* with; does that mean you and Nadia are love's sweet dream after all?'

'After all what?'

Why was she doing this, trying to winkle his personal life with Nadia out of him? It would only hurt more and yet it seemed as compulsive as opening the newspapers on the gossip columns and avidly reading who he was dating now—a sort of media masochism. But she was curious about the two of them. She knew from firsthand knowledge the depth of Mel's passions and yet he gave so little to Nadia in the work environment. Maybe he made up for it in their private life. The thought burned through her painfully. Nadia was having all that should have been hers—his love and caring, his passion and all that was uniquely Mel.

She sipped the wine as she watched him fork prawns in ginger from one of the cartons. He plopped several onto her plate.

'Go on, then, after all what?' he prompted.

Jade took a hesitant breath. Did she really want to know? 'Well, no ring for starters, evasive about a wedding date. She obviously adores you—'

'She's grateful to me,' he interjected, plopping prawns onto his own plate now.

'I expect all your women have been *grateful*,' she retorted sarcastically. 'But what I'm really getting at is your attitude towards her. You're very fond of her, I'm sure, but—'

'Where is all this leading, Jade?'

'I think up the garden path. I'm beginning to wonder about your relationship. I'm beginning to wonder if there is one or if you just invented it to get back at me.' In fact the thought had only just occurred to her.

He smiled thinly. 'Men don't do such things, Jade.'

They did but Jade wasn't going to argue that one; she was onto more interesting things.

'I've watched you with her and I haven't seen much body bonding between you. When we were together you were a very hands-on lover. In fact you find it hard to keep your hands off me even now.' Oh, very risky. She seemed hell-bent on tempting him towards some sort of precipice of admission.

'I did give you an explanation but you don't seem to have grasped it very well.'

'Oh, yes, I remember now,' she drawled sarcastically. 'You were laying ghosts. Well, don't expect to lay the real thing, Mel. Forewarned is forearmed.'

He smiled at her coldly. 'Your forewarned hasn't done much for you yet, sweetheart. You still can't resist me when I take you in my arms.'

Jade stared at him unflinchingly though her poor heart was breaking. 'That was uncalled for,' she muttered miserably.

'That was asked for.' His eyes narrowed to dark slits of warning: Leave this alone or else . . .

He was right, as nearly always. Attacking a prawn with her fingers and teeth, she imagined it was his emotions she was tearing at.

'So, what are these?' she asked, wiping her fingers on a napkin and pulling a sheaf of papers towards her. Work took precedence over emotions and that was what he was here for after all. Be strong, she advised herself.

An hour later they had polished off the prawns, fragrant rice, chicken satay, pork in papaya and lime sauce and most of the wine. They had lost themselves in figures and projections for the following year, but suddenly Mel protested that enough was enough and pushed the paperwork aside. Still sitting at the table, he poured them a last glass of wine and smiled across the debris of the take-away. He looked more relaxed and Jade certainly felt so.

'Just like old times,' he said softly.

Jade couldn't look at him, just stared at the wine in her glass, a slow, hesitant smile softening the tension in her mouth. 'I would have thought you could have come up with something more original than that,' she breathed. She looked up then and the warmth in his eyes hurt her more than his stabbing remarks earlier.

'Touché. Sometimes the old ways are the only ways,' he mused, still holding her eyes deeply and meaningfully.

Jade wondered if she'd detected regret in the remark. She searched the depths of his glittering eyes for confirmation and thought she found it there, but with the wine how could she be sure? She was sure of one thing in her own head, though. She so very deeply regretted what they had lost. They'd had it all, had been perfect for each other four years ago. So deeply in love, wanting each other, laughing so much. Their lives together had been so full of promise and this evening, dining together again, was a mixture of pleasure and pain. How it had been and how it should be but without the promise of more now.

'I'll make coffee,' Jade whispered, and got up from the table to break the unexpected ambience between them. Mel was dangerous in this softer mood and she couldn't trust her own feeble emotions at the moment.

'Do you live here alone?' he asked.

He'd left the table to sit on one of the sofas and while Jade made coffee she took furtive glances at him. It appeared that his softer mood had been dispensed with as swiftly as he had dispensed with her love at her twenty-first birthday party. He picked up magazines from a coffee-table and flicked through them, smoothed his fingers over a tall wooden carving of an Egyptian cat Nicholas had brought back from one of his exotic holidays, and zapped through all the channels on the TV with the remote, finally zapping off altogether. They were all restless movements she wasn't familiar with.

The Mel Biaggio of her past had only ever had eyes for her when they were together, she remembered poignantly. This Mel was fidgety, easily bored and really not very relaxed at all.

As she carried the tray to the coffee-table she reminded herself he wasn't here for pleasure. His pleasure, Nadia, was waiting for him back at home, in his wonderfully elegant apartment overlooking the park. Her heart squeezed at her loss for the millionth time since he'd come back into her life. She'd hoped that aversion therapy would have worked over the weeks but it hadn't. Her heart still twisted when he walked into a room, the sound of his voice on the phone still made her pulse race.

'I never was one of the girls,' she answered, which was a veiled reminder of how close they had been. 'And I told you, I don't have a lover.' She'd told no lies and there was no reason to tell him that Nicholas was here sometimes because he wasn't her lover. Mel wouldn't see that, though, if she did tell him. He hadn't wanted to understand their relationship before and now... now it was none of his business.

'Have you ever had a lover since me?'

The question came out harshly and Jade looked at him in surprise. His eyes were glittery with an anger she hadn't expected to see and she wondered what had prompted it. Revenge again, probably; he was jibing at her, wanting to hurt her more.

Jade forced a smile of defiance. No lovers. Not before and not since and her amorous future would probably be a non-event as well. It was the bit in the middle that Mel had occupied in her life that had ruined it all. He should know but obviously didn't.

'Some ego you have, Mel.' She sat on the sofa across from him, leaning forward to pour the coffee. 'I suppose you think you were so fabulous you couldn't be topped.'

'I recall you once rather naïvely said that, in the heat of one of our moments.'

She checked the rush of heat to her throat at the pointed reminder. Was it possible to stem the hurt? To discuss their past affair rationally and become just friends at the end of it? But a passion like that wasn't the sort to filter into friendship over the years. There could only be bitterness, and yet a while back there hadn't been. She'd seen a softening in his eyes and had imagined regret in his tone, but was she just trying to wish on a star?

'Yes, well, I was rather gauche and overwhelmed by your attentions at the time. I'm older and wiser now.'

'Certainly not more experienced, though.'

Jade leaned back in the sofa with her coffee, fully aware that she was being goaded now. Their work was over—at least all they were willing to put in for the night. She supposed Nadia wasn't due home yet and he had some time to kill so he'd thought he might indulge in a bit of emotion-pricking for fun.

'I don't know, Mel,' she said smoothly. 'I've had my moments.'

None in fact. She'd not even come close to allowing another man in her heart since him; as for allowing one in her bed ... The thought coiled her insides. Mel had been too special a lover for her even to consider it.

'I doubt you've had a single one, Jade,' he said, as if he had just bored into her thoughts and struck at the truth. 'You still react to me the way you used to—sort of endearingly overwhelmed,' he went on. 'Experience with men knocks that out of you. I'd bet my BMW that you've not allowed anyone in your heart since me.'

Oh, how easy it would be to fall into the trap and hurl abuse at him, to give it all away in a flurry of temper, to show that he could hurt her with his true-to-the-bone accusations. But his tone had sounded more regretful than spiteful and because of that she smiled and kept her own tone soft.

'You thought I was married the first day you came to see me, then I was a flirt for eyeing up some guy in the restaurant, and now, apparently, you think I've been leading the life of a nun since you. Make up your mind what you think I am, Mel—not that your opinion matters to me,' she added, just to show she was as strong as he was.

He drank his coffee without a word. She knew he was suddenly angry. His jawline was set, his eyes unblinking now, his fingers far too tight around the Royal Doulton coffee-cup.

She watched him and wondered. Why was he angry with her? Why was he here goading her? Why was he in her life again? He could so easily have walked away that first day in her office. She thought for a moment. Actually he had, as if he had just come to have a morbid peek at a past lover and, satisfied he had no feelings left in that direction, walked away.

But he'd come back and his reasons were obscure. Laying ghosts? Revenge? Or couldn't he stop himself because she was still in his heart? He'd brought Nadia, though, as if to taunt her with his new love, so it must be revenge. But...he could have done the job more thoroughly by openly showing his love for Nadia. He didn't though. He showed affection for Nadia, not the passion he had shown for her during their affair. It was all very confusing.

He put his cup down and glanced at his watch. She wanted him to go yet she didn't. She knew it was hopeless yet...yet hope had never left her; even with Nadia thrust at her she still couldn't believe that Mel belonged to another woman, and certainly not so wholly and completely as to be planning marriage.

'How did you meet Nadia?' she asked softly. What she had really meant to say was, Yes, you'd better go! and with anger in her voice, too, but her changes of mood equalled his at times. Was he as confused as she was?

He smiled and got to his feet. 'I don't think you are really interested.'

'I'm curious; that's near enough.'

'Through a friend of a friend. Now, do you want me to help with the washing-up or would it be safer and wiser if I left now?' His eyes held hers knowingly though Jade hadn't a clue what he was hinting at. And then suddenly she did.

She stood up and the thought thrummed through her that if things weren't the way they were it would be so easy to... what? Ask him to stay? The idea engulfed her like a raging bush fire, nearly fazing her completely. Mel, here in her apartment, Mel in her bed...

Quickly she gathered the coffee-cups together on the tray, her fingers all thumbs. 'I've a dishwasher and I'm quite able to load it on my own,' she told him quickly.

'Good; I never was very domesticated.'

'I remember,' she muttered, crossing to the kitchen area. It hurt to remember. Would it ever not? She scrabbled with the cups and saucers, making too much noise, wanting to drown out the sound of the silly voices in her head which were telling her to make him stay.

'I'll see you tomorrow... Oh, no, you're going to Paris, aren't you?' She'd never been to Paris. If he asked her to go with him, would she? Her sudden desperation must have shown in her eyes because he came round the breakfast bar to her.

'We planned on taking a trip to Paris, remember?'

Jade bit her lip. She looked up at him, eyes wide and brimming, her heart racing so fast it made her breathless. 'The magic carpet,' she whispered. How could she have forgotten? How could he think she had? He'd wanted to whisk her away to romantic Paris on a magic carpet. 'We seem to have done a lot of remembering tonight,' she added mournfully.

'Hurts, doesn't it?'

The edge to his tone told her it was another stab at her.

'It's not incurable,' she told him valiantly, lifting her chin. 'And it doesn't seem to have affected you very much over the years—all those women—'

'Not that many, and amongst the few lucky ones I was looking for what I had lost with you, Jade.'

She got his arrogant meaning straight away. 'You didn't lose anything, Mel, you threw it away. I just hope if the time comes you treat Nadia more fairly than you treated me.'

His eyes narrowed. 'You still feel the hard-done-by one, don't you?'

'I am the hard-done-by one!' she cried in retaliation. 'You are the one able to lead a normal life and...' Her voice gave out. She'd nearly given it away—that she still cared so much for him she'd never be able to lead a normal life.

He grabbed her wrist and pulled her towards him, angry and stiff with tension. 'You think I lead a normal life, do you? You think Nadia could ever be a replacement for you? How little you know me, Jade,' he grazed with contempt. 'If I marry Nadia it won't be for the reason I wanted to marry you four years ago!'

He thrust her away from him and spun around. She watched him gather up a weighty pile of papers and slam them into his briefcase, and yet she felt as if she really wasn't there; her head was spinning with his words. *If* he married Nadia! *He didn't love her!* He hadn't exactly said the words of denial but what he had said meant the same. If he married her it wouldn't be for love—so what *would* it be for, then?

'Are...are you marrying her to punish me?' she asked in a faint whisper, her fists clenched at her sides, her pulses racing so hard she felt sick. The thought was horrendous. If it was true he must hate her so much and want to hurt her so much...

With his hand on the clasp of the briefcase he turned and looked at her, eyes enigmatic, dark and threatening. She'd used to be able to read his moods in his eyes; now he was always a mystery to her.

'Would it punish you if I did?' he asked heavily.

Her eyes squeezed tight shut. How could he ask such a thing? It would be the very end of hope in her life. Marriage would be final to Mel. He was an honourable man; once he made a decision he wouldn't back down on it. In love or not, he'd make the marriage work.

She opened her eyes. 'Your marriage, to whomsoever, would be a blessed release to me,' she told him coldly, and meant it. Finally having Mel out of her life would be a release, like death after a long, debilitating illness.

She went to move past him, to clear the dining table. He was too close and not about to give way. She hesitated nervously and he took her wrist again, this time not in anger. His tender touch unnerved Jade completely.

'And a life sentence to me,' he said under his breath.

The words rang in her ears, discordant at first and then coming across so very clearly. Her eyes widened as he touched the side of her face and then cupped it in his hands and drew her to him. His kiss was confirmation of the meaning of his words and it swelled her heart with hope. He didn't love Nadia; he couldn't love her. She allowed the sweet pressure on her lips because it made all bad reasoning fly from her mind. He didn't love Nadia; he still loved her and wanted her. He couldn't help hurting her with his cruelty and hostility; he was hurting so much himself, it was instinct to lash out.

His lips grew more insistent, tempting her back into his heart, wanting her. His arms, around her back now, held her firmly and yet were not imprisoning her. She could get away if she wanted to and he was giving her the choice. She didn't want to be free, though. She wanted what he was offering—another chance. She wanted it all—him and his love, his heart and all that went with it. The length of his body pressed hard against hers, his passion evident, his need as powerful as hers. His mouth scoured her face and her throat, hot and urgent, making up for so much lost time.

At last he drew back to look down on her swollen lips as he slid open the buttons down the front of her shirt, waiting for some sort of verbal response to what he was doing, exposing her vulnerability, tempting her sexuality as his fingers splayed across her exposed breasts.

She closed her eyes, biting at her lower lip as her breasts swelled under his tender touch. She could only part her lips in silent submission because to speak would be to bring reality flying at her from all sides.

She felt his warm mouth on her nipple and pure sensation coursed down her spine, a delicious feeling that excited and increased her heartbeat till she could hear it drumming in her ears.

'I thought you would have changed,' he whispered huskily against her scented skin. 'But you haven't. It's all exactly as I left it—soft, warm, inviting. Are you inviting me, darling?'

She blinked open her eyes then and, wide and imploring, they stared up at him. How could she answer a question like that when her heart was crying out for so much of him? He made the request sound so simple but it was loaded with complexities, and those complexities were hitting her now, overriding the decision of her heart and putting sense in front of everything else.

'Mel...I don't know...' Confused, she tried to draw back from him, to get space between them to clear her head, but he wouldn't allow it. He held her firmly against him, tempting her with the pressure of need that throbbed between them. She couldn't think when temptation was so close, him so near, crucifying her with a need she had tried so hard to banish from her soul.

'You know that I want you,' he murmured. 'The passion is still there for us, after all this time, and—'

'And it would be wrong to give in to it, Mel,' she implored faintly, her legs like jelly, scarcely able to hold her up. She struggled for words, honest words. 'I...I want you too but, Mel, it isn't just us.'

'Nadia?'

She lowered her spinning head. The mention of her name was enough to engulf her with shame. This betrayal of Nadia for her own selfish reasons, her love and need for Mel, was all wrong.

'And yet four years ago—'

She didn't let him finish. She willed her hands up and pushed at his chest, her fists small and powerless against his hard strength. The futility of it all angered her as he held her ever more strongly.

Her eyes shot poison at him because it was all she had to fight him with. She seethed at him through thin lips of anger, 'You still think there was something between me and Nicholas and you will never accept that there wasn't. If there had been, I'd be married to him now. And suggesting that I go to bed with you now because I was supposedly a two-timer then is despicable.' She took a ragged breath. 'Yes, I want you—how can I deny it when you know it?—but wanting and having isn't possible, not with you, Mel. You have Nadia now and—'

'She doesn't wear my ring—'

She punched his chest then, small, ineffectual thumps that got her nowhere. 'What's a damned ring? Nothing, Mel. You've made the commitment—'

'There is no commitment,' he grated, almost angrily, as if she was at fault and not him. 'Not yet,' he added with a weight that stiffened the whole of her body into numbness and stilled her clenched fists against his shirtfront.

'I...I don't understand,' she whispered faintly. Her head was swimming. She couldn't have heard right, surely? If she had, the implication of it didn't bear thinking about.

His eyes darkened moodily, almost closing off a part of himself he didn't want probed. 'You don't have to understand, Jade,' he whispered passionately. 'All you need to know is that I want to make love to you and I wouldn't think of it if I was formally committed to another woman.'

'Yes, but...' But still she didn't understand, not fully. He had said that he was betrothed that first time he'd come to her in her office. Had he said it to punish her? At the sight of her after so long had all the supposed betrayal he had suffered four years ago welled up inside him, firming him with a need to punish her? Now he was saying he was not committed to Nadia—'not yet'. If she refused him would he propose to Nadia?

'Please let me go, Mel,' she whispered, confused out of her mind. Was he forcing her to make the choice for him, her or Nadia?

'I can't let you go, not this time,' he grated roughly.

She tried to turn her head away from him but he stopped her with firm fingers securing her chin. A sob caught in her throat, a deep sob of release, and there were tears pricking the backs of her eyes which suddenly spilled over, blurring her vision.

'Oh, Mel,' she breathed weakly. 'What's happening to us? What have we done and what are we doing to ourselves now?'

The answer was in his mouth on hers, claiming her passionately, his arms enfolding her, securing her as if never to let her go. She knew then that this was no act. She felt the passion surging through him and knew that no amount of deviousness could sham that. He still wanted her and she him and what was to become of them?

Jade held him tight, wanting no one in the world to exist but themselves. She wouldn't think of that fateful night four years back; she wouldn't think of the pain and suffering they had both endured since. Mel wanted her and she had never stopped wanting him.

Suddenly he scooped her up into his arms and she clung to him, burying her face in his neck. Her heart led her. In total resignation she murmured his name and it was all that needed to be said.

CHAPTER SEVEN

IT HAD been far too long. Nervousness sent shock waves down the backs of Jade's legs as Mel set her down in her bedroom. The light from the small hallway off the main living area was all the light in the room and Jade wished she had switched it off. She was overwhelmed with a shyness she had never experienced before with him.

Mel switched on a soft bedside light, closed the bedroom door and then took her in his arms again. His kisses were light and feathery on her brow and down the side of her face, soft, warm kisses of reassurance. 'You're trembling,' he murmured. 'Don't be afraid, sweet one. Nothing has changed.'

But it had. They had both suffered so terribly and now they might not know each other. They were different people, influenced and changed by their pain. Doubt rushed at her, dissolving all her confidence till she clung to him, her arms tight around his neck, her fevered mouth seeking his for the guidance she needed. And then her heart swelled with love for him as he closed his mouth fully over hers and she knew she had nothing to fear. When you loved so deeply there was no room for doubt.

Very tenderly Mel pushed her shirt back over her shoulders and it slid to the ground. He groaned helplessly as he ran his hands over her naked breasts, and when he lowered his mouth to her hot, scented skin she felt ecstasy engulf her like a sheet of moving fire. His tongue and lips tantalised her to the edge of endurance,

teasing across her breast, rushing over her swollen
nipples, arousing her so heatedly and swiftly that her
legs felt as if they were melting.

He lifted her and she seemed to float on air and then
slowly descended to the deep softness of her duvet. She
moaned softly and fluttered open her eyes and the man
she loved and adored was gazing down at her. His dark,
dark Italian eyes were hooded and heavy with such deep
desire that her mouth parted, inviting him down into the
depth of her love and passion.

She watched him slowly undress in front of her, each
movement so smooth and seductive that she wondered
if he practised the art. And it was an art—his body was
a work of art, so muscled and dark and mysterious. She
reached out to him as he discarded his silk boxer shorts,
anxious to touch him and help him and be a part of him.

His breath caught roughly in his throat as she touched
him intimately, taking him in her hands and leaning up
to kiss the warm, silken, aroused skin. He pressed against
her with another moan and then shuddered and drew
back from her.

He sank down beside her on the bed and loosened her
skirt and tossed it aside. He bent and kissed her tiny lace
pants and then eased them away from her fiery skin and
his mouth grazed heatedly above the triangle of dark
hair.

The heat of his mouth, the fierceness of his breathing
made her press her fingers into his back, urging him to
her. It would have been so easy to lose control, to let
their animal need take over and consummate their love
out of mere expediency. But both were aware of the
preciousness of their lovemaking, and the need to
prolong the sweet pleasure outweighed the urgency.

Her own lips scored across his, her desire, so openly
displayed, arousing him even more till both were barely

hanging onto reality. It was a dream-like time in which
Jade could only revel in her deep love for him. She
touched and aroused his magnificent body and wondered at such strength. Tears filled her eyes as she
thought of all the pain she had put him through, thought
of this strong, powerful man suffering because of his
own pride and stubbornness. And she hadn't been strong
enough to help him and not strong enough to help herself
either.

But that was past and the present was heady and overwhelmingly sensuous. They were together again and
nothing mattered but the here and now. Being together,
loving each other.

He kissed her deeply, his fingers blazing trails of white
fire on her receptive skin. She twisted against him wan-
tonly as he stroked her sensitive inner thighs and the
need inside her rose furiously till her breath caught in
her throat. There was fire on fire as his tender explo-
ration deepened, taking her up and beyond and into a
world that was only theirs. Love and eroticism, sensuality and need, Jade lost herself in it all, Mel loving her,
Mel needing her, Mel her life.

Neither could hold back any longer. He rose above
her like some magnificent beast, male and dark and
predatory in his urgency for her. With a small cry of
desire she arched against him as he thrust into her, so
strong, his breathing deep as his heat moved inside her.
He had complete control over her heart, her senses, her
fragile body. He supported her hips with one strong
hand, moving into her with long, fluid strokes that
caused such an intensity of feeling to surge through her
that she gasped.

'You're mine again,' he breathed raggedly.

For one painful second the words stabbed at her,
sounding to her weakened senses as if his possession of

her was indeed revenge, but then the uncertainty flew as if it had wings. This wasn't revenge. This was Mel loving her because he had always loved her and couldn't stop loving her now. Her fragile emotions soared too, hope and desire swelling her heart until she felt as if it might burst at any moment.

Jade cried out and clung to him as their climax broke, shuddering their bodies together, a fury of heat vibrating through them as the pressure exploded.

Wave after wave of sensation careered between them and they clung to each other as they rode the waves, crest after crest, till there was no more turbulence, only sweet, smooth rushes of billowing warmth and a bonding that was inescapable. They were as one, Jade and Mel, as they would always be.

They lay exhausted in each other's arms, trying to level their breathing, trying to calm down sufficiently to be able to speak. But no words would come. It had all been said in their kisses and their lovemaking. They couldn't live without each other any more.

'I have to go,' she heard Mel murmur, and the words hit Jade where it hurt most—her sensitive heart.

She sat bolt upright in bed, an instinctive reaction as if she'd been doused with cold water. She raked her tousled hair from her face, praying she had been mistaken in thinking there was an edge to his tone. After the wondrous night how could there be?

Still dazed with sleep, her body limp and aching as a reminder of what had happened the night before, she focused her misty eyes on him. Dear God, but he was showered and dressed and leaving. Her heart thudded.

'Mel,' she husked, her throat unbearably tight and painful.

He looked down at her, eyes unreadable, his voice barely audible. 'Paris, remember? I have to make a dash for the airport.'

There was an unbearable rough edge to his low tone, as if he couldn't wait to get away and she was holding him up. Jade stared at him in disbelief, her heart so cold inside her that she thought it would surely freeze. No warmth this morning from him. She had expected to wake up in his arms, with him holding her and pressing warm kisses to her brow; she had imagined he'd want to talk—about their second chance, the love that had survived four years of abstinence—but there was nothing but cold dismissal in his tone and his dark, accusing eyes.

'You're angry,' she blurted, willing her legs out of the bed so that she could face him. But willing her legs to move wasn't enough. She was paralysed with fear and confusion. Last night he had been so wonderful, this morning so...so...

'Only with myself,' he uttered icily. 'The cold light of day and all that.'

'Mel!' She was aware that she had screamed his name. Life came back to her legs and she flew from the bed, naked and shivering, not able to take this in. What had happened? Last night... Her heart missed a million beats. Colour rushed to her face. Numbly she reached for a robe at the foot of the bed. Mel didn't love her. Mel had punished her, used her. Mel had taken his revenge. He couldn't forgive and forget. Images of Nadia rushed at her from all sides, flooding her with a guilt that should have flooded her when Mel had been making love to her. Oh, God, what was happening to her?

'M-Mel, we...we have to talk,' she stammered helplessly.

He glanced at his watch and her heart pounded so painfully that she swayed. He couldn't even bring himself to look her in the eye. Anger surged within her then, a bitterness that almost foamed in her mouth. He had used her in the worst possible way. Coldly and cruelly he had punished her for what he thought she had done to him four years ago. She wanted to plead but the words wouldn't come to her stricken throat. She stood helpless and small by the bed, trembling inside, diminished to almost nothing because she had allowed this to happen.

He looked at her then, with eyes so hostile that she nearly let her heart leap with irrational hope. If he had made love to her as an act of revenge he should be looking triumphant, not hostile. And he wasn't triumphant, not at all. Just coldly angry with her. Or was he angry with himself for letting his emotions run away with him? If so there was a chance, but she couldn't ask, she just couldn't force the words from her trembling white lips.

'I'll call from Paris,' he said, and they were his final words, cruelly final. He turned and, shoulders stiff with tension, walked out of the bedroom.

The door slammed behind him and Jade flinched. The walls seemed to close in on her, squeezing the very life from her lungs, leaving her breathless and gasping for air. Then she started to shake, nature's way of revival, shocking her back into the real world. Mel was gone. He'd left without a word of love. Coldly and clinically he had walked out of her life again.

Her head was thumping and her skin felt raw. She forced herself to move out of the bedroom, as if she might find the answer to the world's mysteries in another room. Oh, God, what had happened to Mel to change him from the sensuous lover of the night before to this very devil of cold hostility this morning? she wondered despairingly.

The walls of the vast open-plan living area seemed to close in on her too, narrowing her focus. And then she saw something she hadn't seen the night before. Something she should have seen. Across the back of a chair, in a corner by the opening to the inner hall, hung a dry cleaner's bag.

Jade approached it hesitantly, as if it might spring up and snatch at her throat. She stood by it, staring down at it till her eyes were dark pools of distress. The label with the name 'Fields' clearly scrawled on it mocked her and her head swam till she felt sick with realisation. Mel had seen it. It was so obvious now. He had rightly jumped to the conclusion that Nicholas was living here, but whether he'd seen it last night or this morning *wasn't* obvious to her tangled senses. Had he known last night and made love to her for pure revenge? Her heart clenched at the thought.

Jade bit her lip punishingly. Or was it worse? Had Mel only seen it this morning and felt irrevocably hurt and betrayed yet again? Yes, that was worse, for Mel, that he might think she was no better than he thought her four years ago.

Jade sobbed out a strangled curse at Trisha for not putting the suits away, she cursed Nicholas for being in her life, and then last and more importantly she cursed herself for being such a fool. She should have told him. How could she have made the same mistake a second time in her life?

In a daze of misery Jade rushed to Nicholas's bedroom and flung open the door. It was obvious the room was used by a man and Mel might have seen it, seeking further evidence after finding the suits, in which case wouldn't he have realised that though Nicholas might be living here he wasn't sharing her bed? Didn't he realise after last night that *he*, Mel Biaggio, was the only love of her life and had always been the only love for her?

Her misery was unparalleled, so much worse than anything she'd experienced before. 'It's enough that he believes he's still in my life,' Jade breathed out loud with anguish. 'He's programmed that way, damn him, programmed by pride, with no room for reasoning.' She let out a sob of grief and anger. He wouldn't listen if she tried to explain. Just as he hadn't listened before, so what was the point? Last time it had taken him only seconds to blow her out of his life, this time only marginally longer.

With another sob of anguish Jade tried to imagine what revengeful measure he would take in the future, because he wouldn't let this go, that was for sure. She had injured him even more, damaged herself beyond repair. There was no hope now—nothing, nothing. She was devastated and there was only one way to go.

She took hold of herself, straightened her emotions till they were taut against more pain. She was determined now the initial shock was over. She'd come out of this with her sanity intact if nothing else. Mel wouldn't listen to reason; it was hopeless, and that was a thought to keep firmly in mind. Last night had been an aberration and aberrations were best put behind you. Life had to go on.

Miserably Jade stared through the glass doors of the studio, unobtrusively watching the bubbly Nadia at work. David was leaning over her board and they were laughing together. How could people laugh when life was such a terrible pain? It was all so much harder to deal with than her determination had led her to believe.

'Two more calls this morning,' Diane told Jade when she returned to the office. 'I keep telling these people

Mel is in Paris and you'll speak to them, but it's Mel they want. Can't blame them,' she added dreamily. 'He is gorgeous.'

'Women!' Jade snapped. 'Have women been calling him here?' So he hadn't changed. There were others as well as her and Nadia. Her hand went to her forehead and she kneaded her brow.

Diane eyed her curiously. 'Not all of them were women, but...but they *were* business calls. Marshall Osbourne in particular—several calls from him.'

Jade's hand dropped to her side and a small prickle snatched at her spine. She picked up a pile of faxes from Diane's desk and swept into her office, muttering under her breath, 'They were probably at kindergarten together.'

Diane heard and laughed but Jade wasn't laughing when she slammed her door. Just what the hell did Mel Biaggio think he was doing? Anyone would think he ran this company now!

She slumped down at her desk and for a moment held her head in her hands to get herself together. She was almost glad of this new development; it was a diversion to narrow her thinking to the company rather than Mel. If what she was thinking was true it would help her heart to get back to some semblance of normality. She picked up the phone and dialled Marshall's number. Ritchie's had done his advertising for years. He was a friend of her father's. What could he have to say to Mel that she couldn't deal with?

Ten minutes later she knew and it was what she had suspected.

In a fury Jade stormed into Diane's office. 'Any calls that come through for Mel you put through to me. If anyone refuses you tell them straight that this is not Mel Biaggio's company, it's mine! Mel Biaggio has no con-

nection with this company other than as a consultant!
Mel Biaggio is—'

'Back,' came from the door as it swung open.

Jade glared at him angrily, refusing to acknowledge
how drained and haggard he looked. He'd probably
heard her screams of anguish down on the ground floor.
Well, if he cared to step into her office, he'd hear them
all over again—even louder!

She didn't even have to ask. He strode past her, dark
and menacing and very travel-weary, straight into the
office. Jade followed, slamming the door after her.

'Leave that coffee alone,' she ordered. 'That is *my*
coffee. This is *my* office. This is *my* company and—'

'Your father's company,' he corrected her frostily.
'Calm down, Jade. And remember you'd be facing your
father with a winding-up order now if it wasn't for me.
What's all this about?' He poured coffee with his back
to her, that broad back that she had clung to so passionately... It didn't bear thinking about. She couldn't—
no, wouldn't—allow him to get into her heart again.

Jade clenched her fists to steady herself. She was
furious with him and knew that allowing her senses to
go off on an emotional tangent was weak and pointless.
He was an arrogant swine, she reminded herself, and
clever too, but not clever enough to cheat her out of her
heart *and* her company.

'It's all about you having everyone believing you run
this company now!' she told him. 'Marshall Osbourne,
one of my oldest clients, my father's before me, is ringing
this office asking for you and not me. And there have
been others before him, all wanting to speak to you...
I rang Marshall and he said he'd heard rumours that we
are... we are...'

Oh, no, her voice was giving out. Mel was back from
Paris, here in her office, facing her now as she hurled

out abuse at the way he was taking over. Oh, yes, she
was mad about that, but if he stepped towards her and
took her in his arms and told her he loved her... Oh,
God, he was staring at her so coldly and unemotionally.
He *did* believe she was living with Nicholas and she
should never have allowed that to happen. And now
where was her grim determination to get over him when
she needed it?

'Go on, don't run out of steam; you can do it,' he
urged, as if he were prompting a foreign language
student. His expression didn't change. Cold and hostile,
he waited for her response.

Jade ran her tongue over her dry lips. Suddenly, ir-
rationally, she didn't want to talk about the company.
She wanted to talk about them, to try to reason with
him once again. Over and over again she had tried to
convince herself that Mel wasn't such a monster as to
be able to make love to her simply out of revenge and
she had nearly succeeded. Almost convinced herself that
he couldn't have done it without feeling.

Now, however, as she stared at him, she wasn't sure,
and it reinforced her theory that this whole situation was
hopeless. She really was fighting a losing battle but again
and again a spurt of hope struggled to the surface and
made her say and do things she had resolved not to. Like
now—she was letting the way he looked at her unfold
her hardened emotions to expose her vulnerability.

'Mel, it isn't what it seems,' she said plaintively.

He frowned. 'What isn't?' he asked in a tone that im-
plied he genuinely didn't know.

But Jade knew he did. He was getting some sort of
morbid pleasure out of putting her through this. And
she couldn't take any more punishment; enough was
enough. She had to be harder, stronger, as hard and as
noncommittal as he. With an enormous effort she lifted

her chin and returned his coolness with her own. This
wasn't the time or the place to thrash out their love life.
She had to get company business dealt with before
thinking of her personal pain. She took a deep breath.

'Marshall said he'd heard rumours that there was going
to be a change of ownership. He said you had led him
to believe—'

'I can't be made accountable for what other people
believe, Jade,' he told her evenly.

'You've met him. He said you put a new advertising
suggestion to him, something completely different, and
he got the impression—'

'Whatever impressions he got have no bearing on me,'
he said darkly. He went to his desk with his coffee and
Jade wanted to knock it out of his hands with frustration. He had an answer to everything.

She crossed the room and stood in front of his desk
as he sat down, her eyes narrowed warningly. 'I want
you out of this company and—'

'Out of your life, no doubt,' he interjected lethally.

Jade's heart wrenched. What if she said she didn't
want him out of her life, that she wanted him in it and
for it to be like it was before Nicholas and Nadia and
the world had intervened? She saw the cold determination in his Italian eyes. She might as well fight World
War Three on her own with a bent pitchfork, it was that
hopeless, she realised.

'You were out of my life four years ago, Mel,' she
said. 'You wouldn't listen then and nothing has changed.
Our night of love last week was your revenge and—'

'We're getting personal here now, are we?' he drawled.

His tone was so blatantly mocking that she fought back
immediately because it was the only way to stop herself
crumbling before him. 'Don't play idiotic games, Mel,
not now. The joke is beginning to wear thin. Your re-

venge pitch was very funny, I don't think!' she grazed sarcastically.

He shot to his feet, fire brightening his eyes. 'My revenge!' he blazed. 'I'm sick of hearing that word bandied around as if you think I base my life on it. You, always you, the hurt one—'

'I know what you're thinking, that's why!' she cried.

'If you lived for ever you'd never know what I'm thinking because you only think of your own supposed hurt. My pain doesn't exist!'

'I...I want to explain.'

'And I don't want to hear some feeble protestation that I must be mistaken and you are *not* living with Nicholas Fields—'

'Don't be ridiculous!' Jade cried. 'I don't take you for a fool, Mel.'

His eyes blackened murderously. 'But you do—you have! Not once but twice! Nicholas Fields drove us apart four years ago and you didn't learn, did you? For God's sake you're living with the man and probably have been since for ever!'

'It's not what it seems!' Jade protested hotly, and even as the words came out she knew they were a hopeless repetition of her earlier protests. He would never listen to reason.

'So for some obscure reason he chooses to store his suits in your apartment, or perhaps you had simply picked them up for him and—'

'No, Mel!' Jade pleaded. 'Please—'

'"No, Mel"?' he echoed in rage, and shot round the desk to her. Jade flinched as he gripped her shoulders fiercely, as if he wanted to shake the life from her. 'Thank God I had to leave for Paris that morning because if I had stayed you might not be here now, trying to make pathetic excuses for yet another betrayal. I've had a week to get myself together over this,' he grated fiercely. 'I always did suspect you might be my life sentence, but I'm not going to spend it inside for the likes of you so don't tremble in my arms as if you fear for your life.'

'I'm trembling with anger, not fear,' Jade flamed back, trying to shake his powerful hands from her shoulders but failing miserably. 'You never let me explain; you won't allow me to put my side of it. Nicholas has a girl-friend and—'

'*Ménage à trois?* That wouldn't surprise me given the circles you move in!'

'You don't know the circles I move in because you have never wanted to know,' she fought back. 'You are so damned old-fashioned I'm amazed at your woman-ising reputation.' Her eyes narrowed, lending intensity to what she was saying. 'I'm not even going to waste my breath trying to explain my living arrangement with Nicholas but I would like to stress one point you might like to give thought to at some time. Sex is so high on your list of priorities with women that—'

'You think this is about sex?' he stormed, letting her go so abruptly that she swayed. Fists clenched at his sides, he stood before her, unremitting, unrelenting, un-merciful. 'You even insult my intelligence to the very end. Can't you see your betrayal goes deeper than merely sexual? It's enough that you have a life with this man; it's enough that he is in your life when I was deprived of the chance. Can't you see that?'

'No, I can't,' she breathed raggedly. 'You have Nadia and—'

'I wasn't involved with Nadia four years ago when I was in love with you,' he interrupted. 'Why did you keep Nicholas from me four years ago? Why is he still in your life to this day if he doesn't mean anything to you? Do you get some sort of perverted pleasure out of running around with two men?'

'Stop it!' Jade cried desperately, her fists tightly clenched. How could he torture her this way? It was so cruel and so unfair. Why wouldn't he listen?

'Why didn't you tell me the second time around?' he went on, unrelenting in his pursuit of further revenge. 'You had the opportunity. In my bloody innocence I even asked you if you shared your apartment!'

Jade gazed at him in dismay, her eyes wide, deep pools of despair. Yes, he had given her the opportunity and she hadn't seized it and that had been her big mistake. And then he had been approachable and now he wasn't because she had let it go too far. She parted her lips, not knowing where to begin to try and explain yet again, but the buzz of her intercom jarred her senses into life. Automatically she reached for it but Mel was quicker, his hand snaking out and grasping her wrist. In defiance she flashed her dark eyes at him and reached for the intercom with her other hand.

'Nicholas on the line for you, Jade. I told him you were busy but he says it's important.'

Mel's grip on Jade's wrist burned like a sadistic Chinese torture and his eyes were slivers of ice, and Jade knew with a desperately sinking heart that she had made yet another appalling mistake in insisting on answering the intercom. And what appalling timing on Nicholas's part. He couldn't have picked a worse moment to ring her.

She stared back at Mel, her whole body slackened in defeat, her eyes bleak. From somewhere came her voice, flat and dead, as if someone else were forming the words for her and projecting them through her pale lips. 'I'll call him back, Diane,' she instructed dully.

'I wonder what was so important?' he breathed sarcastically as he thrust her wrist contemptuously away from him. 'What's for supper tonight, maybe?'

She clutched at her wrist, rubbed where he had gripped it and slowly and composedly she closed her heart to him, locking it all away—her smashed emotions and aching senses and every reason for ever loving him. There was only one way to go, one direction she could take. She stepped back from him, lifted her chin and her eyes were glacial as she spoke meaningfully and forcefully.

'I want you and your baggage off my premises immediately. Take your talent, Nadia, and the two of you get out of this company. Send me a bill for your services, Mel. Whatever the price I'll pay it, even if I have to sell all my worldly goods, because I will not be indebted to you!'

He watched her as she spoke, watched her lips moving and her eyes so hard and determined, and when she'd finished he moved back around his desk, separating them as if it was important that he did so. Then he smiled. A smile she could happily have sliced off his face with the cutting edge of her tongue if she could have thought of something further to floor him with.

'You have a lot to learn about me, Jade Ritchie,' he said quietly and damningly. 'You don't tell me when to come and go and you don't tell me what to do with the women in my life. I'm here to stay for as long as it takes. As for Nadia, she answers to me, not you. I stay. She stays. As for you...' His index finger came up warningly and his eyes narrowed to slivers of steel. 'You, Jade Ritchie, walk a dangerous path every time you cross mine. Here, in this office, we talk business and nothing else. We don't have a personal life any more. You very successfully destroyed that, as you are so adept at doing. Have I made myself clear?'

Jade's world seemed to close in on her, crushing her very soul. They hadn't a chance and probably never had had if she cared to punish herself more by thinking of it in depth. Because of her grave error in not telling him about Nicholas, she had ruined any chance of reconciliation with Mel.

But she wasn't entirely to blame. He must take some of it onto his own shoulders—but of course he wouldn't. He was always right and she was always wrong. Nothing had ever got through his thick mantle of pride. Not her love, then or now, although she had shown it so clearly the night they had made love, shown how deeply she cared for him, how right they were for each other. All hopeless. She'd torn her emotions ragged since he'd come back into her life, and for what? Nothing but pain and more sorrow. And now he was throwing his weight around in her business world as well as her emotional life, *commanding* her to obey him.

He was ten times more powerful than she had imagined, she realised, her heart thudding dully. He almost struck fear into her, but fear wasn't what she needed in her life now and she wouldn't allow him to frighten her this way. This was still her father's company, not his, and she was plugging into that source of power and would use it and gain from it. She would use Mel Biaggio in a professional way, as had been the original intention.

Determinedly she squared her shoulders and looked at him unflinchingly. 'Yes, you've made yourself clear, Mel,' she said strongly and levelly. 'Do what you do best—save the company—because you are pretty useless at everything else. Just allow me this last word on our personal life—and it will be the last, I promise you. Our relationship didn't stand a chance from the off, Mel, because you are so obstinately old-fashioned. You can't hold a woman and you never will,' she went on with feeling. 'I've a feeling Nadia will turn you down in the end. She will if she has any sense, anyway, because you—you are a tyrant!'

She hadn't got to him as she had intended, hadn't managed to hurt him in retaliation for all the hurt he had doused her with. She could tell by the way the corners of his mouth turned up that she hadn't even grazed his emotions. With one last look of contempt fired at her from across the room, he turned and left the office. And as always left Jade with a feeling that whatever she said or did he would always, but always come out on top.

She stared at the door, every ounce of will in her body fighting the need to crumble into a heap of despair. How could he fill her with such fury one moment and the next reduce her to some wretched weak and ineffectual idiot? The trouble was, it was hard to hurt a brick wall, unless you were another brick wall—and Jade wasn't. At this moment she felt as feeble as an out-of-date lettuce leaf. Weakly she slumped down into her chair and took a long, ragged breath, trying to gather her senses.

'Mel stormed out in a fury,' Diane told her as she stepped into the office. 'Sorry, did I interrupt delicate negotiations with Nicholas's call?'

Jade looked up and managed a very thin, rueful smile. 'No, nothing important.' Only her life, the destruction of it, she added silently. No, to hell with Mel Biaggio; he hadn't completely put her down yet. She was going to come out of this if it killed her.

Diane looked relieved. 'Nicholas said not to bother calling back, he'd sort it out for himself.'

'Sort what out?' Jade asked, her life back on automatic pilot.

'His supper.' Diane laughed. 'Men are unbelievable at times, aren't they?' She gathered up some artwork from Jade's desk and bounced out again.

Yes, men were unbelievable—small-minded, narrow-minded, pigheaded. And the contender for all those titles was Mel Biaggio. Diane knew she lived with Nicholas on a friendly basis, accepted it because that was how it was in the real world. Diane herself shared a house with two men and another girl. The trouble was, Mel didn't live in the real world. He lived on another planet.

Jade's tears came then, for Mel's hurt pride, for all the misunderstandings she couldn't resolve. She would allow herself a cry now and be done with it, because it would be the last time she shed a tear over him.

Two minutes and it was all over. She crumpled a tissue in her hand and flung it determinedly into the bin, then stood up and went to the window. She was still standing there half an hour later.

CHAPTER EIGHT

MEL and Jade, seated at their desks across the room from each other, waited till Nadia had closed the door behind her then spoke at once, Jade's voice raised heatedly and Mel's showing more control.

'How dare you?'

'It's the only way!' Mel held up a warning hand and Jade gritted her teeth. 'Cool it, Jade, and listen to reason—'

'I'm always open to reason,' Jade blurted with frustration. 'But you're not capable of it. You have to dominate. You have to override every point of view I put forward. I've been running this company and—'

'And let it run down,' Mel interjected quietly and levelly.

As he was forever telling her, outbursts of temper got them nowhere. But it was a blessed release, Jade had argued, except that lately she hadn't got that expected rush of release after firing off at him.

She was crumbling, that was why. She couldn't cope with Nadia. Nadia wasn't the 'other woman' she should be. She was sweet and talented and Jade knew that they would be great friends if it wasn't for Mel. Guilt swamped her every time she faced Nadia, a terrible nagging guilt for what had happened that night in her apartment.

But every time she thought about it she reasoned that she hadn't been in her right mind and that if Mel and Nadia's relationship had been stronger she would have never allowed it to happen. Nadia adored Mel, but did she love him? Were they truly committed to each other, committed enough for marriage? Mel had talked his way out of that one but it was all so confusing.

Mel Biaggio was winning. Undoubtedly with her company, undoubtedly with her emotions. There were times she couldn't think straight and others when her thinking was dead on line, like today.

'OK,' she agreed, calmly now because it was the only way—his way. 'Let's discuss this rationally and—'

'Without allowing our personal feelings to get in the way,' he interrupted yet again.

Her eyes pleaded with his across the wide expanse of office space between them. 'Mel, this *is* personal,' she insisted. 'It can't be anything else. You and Nadia are undermining me, and because of your relationship with each other it has got to affect your judgement.'

'I'm doing this for the company, Jade,' he reasoned. 'It isn't personal. I'm doing a job of work and Nadia's idea is good, and if you can't see that you shouldn't be in this business.'

Jade shot to her feet. Sometimes she couldn't bear to face him, and one of those times was now. She stood by the window, glaring out at the world, her arms wrapped around herself for comfort because she was the only one available.

She hated dealing with them together; it made her feel at a disadvantage. Mel and Nadia, side by side, against her. It hurt her immeasurably but there was no choice but to endure it.

'Marshall Osbourne will reject the idea, Mel,' she told him coolly. 'I don't want you to submit the presentation to them. We've always done their advertising and they've always been satisfied in the past. I see no point in changing a winning formula for something so... so avant-garde.'

'You are against it because it came from Nadia. If Dave had come up with the idea—'

She swung around then and glowered at him. 'No, Mel, you're wrong! I'm trying not to take this personally. I really am trying to detach myself from the fact that you and Nadia are—'

'And yet your pinched little face is pressed against that very window every night, watching us leaving together,' he scathed so unmercifully that Jade's heart squeezed with the hurt. 'What a little hypocrite you are, rushing home to your Nicholas every night and pretending that the sight of me and Nadia together actually gets to you.'

She shook her head in dismay, fighting her pain. Would it never end? 'You don't lose out on any opportunity to hurt me, Mel,' she whispered hoarsely, her throat clogged with emotion. 'You might think you're clever but you only show your true ignorance. Cruelty isn't clever, Mel. It shows weakness, not strength of character.'

His eyes were steady as he gazed across at her. 'Were you speaking those words to me or were you telling yourself something?' His lips thinned. 'I'm here to help your company, not to put you down as you think. The quicker you accept that, the quicker I can get this business rolling safely enough to get out of your life.'

'And will you take Nadia with you?' she questioned flintily, her heart secretly tearing at the thought of him going for good. Despite these arguments, despite the sometimes stifling tension between them, she knew if she really was free of him the sense of loss she would feel would be worse than before. Why was love so irrational? She ought to be praying for the day he went instead of dreading it. 'If you go, will she go? Or perhaps you'll leave her here, to carry on the torture after you've gone. I wouldn't put that past you.'

'You see, you can't help but take this personally,' he sighed in exasperation.

Oh, she couldn't get it right with him. She was straining to hold onto her temper and not having a lot of success. If she didn't get out of this office she would explode. Crossing the room, she snatched Nadia's artwork up from Mel's desk.

She scowled at him. 'If you won't tell her I will.'

'No, Jade!'

She was off and running before he could catch another breath. Diane helped, though unwittingly, by stopping him in the outer office with an accounts file and a very urgent query that Jade didn't wait to hear about.

'I'm sorry, Nadia,' she began a few minutes later, placing the artwork carefully on Nadia's drawing board. She was aware of the other woman tensing slightly and tried to make her rejection as painless as possible. 'It's marvellous work but I'm afraid I'm not able to submit the idea—'

'But Mel said my ideas were brilliant,' Nadia protested, her very dark lashes fluttering impatiently.

Jade clenched her fists at her sides. This was how far things had gone since Mel had brought her into the agency. A couple of weeks ago Nadia wouldn't have said boo to a goose. Now she was calling the shots in Jade's agency, as if she and Mel owned it! So how to handle this blossoming of Mel's lover—put her down immediately and tell her in no uncertain terms who was the boss here? And show herself to be jealous! she realised grimly.

Jade swallowed and forced a smile because her emotions couldn't suffer another loss of face. 'And Mel is right—the idea is brilliant and I know you've put a lot of work into it, but I know from past experience that

Marshal Osbourne won't go for it. His is an old estab-
lished company and he and his colleagues won't go for
such drastic changes in their advertising.'

'Jade, advertising and marketing techniques are
changing all the time,' Nadia reasoned determinedly.
'Why don't you put it to them and see how they take
it?'

Jade clenched her fists even more tightly. Nadia was
gaining confidence, with guidance from Mel, no doubt.
Where was it going to end?

'Because it will be a waste of time—'

'Why not give it a try, Jade?' Mel said smoothly from
behind them.

Jade and Nadia swung round to face him. Jade's eyes
flicked furiously from one to the other; she felt trapped
and put upon and so terribly out of everything.

'To have it slammed back in our faces, Mel? Because
that is what will happen. I know these people—'

'Don't forget I've had talks with Marshall—'

It was the conciliatory tone that did it for Jade, as if
all her four years' work in the agency accounted for
nothing and all that mattered now was this
damned…damned brilliant idea of Nadia's. Resentment
at having to endure weeks of his put-downs welled up
inside her. She couldn't bear it any more. He was destroying her very soul.

'Damn you, Mel Biaggio!' she cried in frustration.
She grasped at the sketches on Nadia's drawing board
and thrust them into Mel's chest. 'Take them, submit
them. What does it matter what I say or do? I've no…no
authority here…I'm…I'm…'

To her horror and shame she burst into tears.
Impossibly the tears streamed down her face and she
couldn't have stopped them if she'd tried. Ashamed at
her weakness and through a blur of red mist, she swung

away from them both and hurtled towards the door, wanting to be far away from the two of them, far away from everyone and everything.

She felt her arm being seized but ploughed on nevertheless, driven by despair, not able to shake away the grip on her arm. There was nowhere to run to without prying eyes. Dazed with confusion, everything a blur through her tears, she hesitated at the stairwell, unsteady on her high heels, and then she was steadied by the support of two strong hands on her shoulders. She was gently urged down to the ground floor and through the double doors of the new presentation suite, which was nearly complete and mercifully empty.

Through an echo chamber of despair she heard the doors slam behind them and then Mel tried to fold her into his arms and she sobbed and gasped and struggled against him, bringing her small, bunched fists up to pound ineffectually against the brick wall of his chest.

'I hate you, Mel Biaggio, I hate you!' she sobbed in anguish. And she did—hated him for all he had put her through, then and now and for ever. There was no let-up in his cold dismissal of her heart and her ideas—and everything!

He held her firmly yet allowed her enough freedom to work her anger into a state of exhaustion, and eventually she collapsed against him, weak and senseless with spent rage, and he stroked her silky hair with long strokes, trying to comfort and calm her. 'No, you don't and that's the trouble,' he murmured tenderly.

She pushed at him then, with the little strength she had left, and lifted her burning, tear-streaked face to glare at him defiantly. 'I do hate you, Mel,' she insisted hoarsely. 'At this precise moment in time I hate you for everything. I hate you for taking on this job, for thrusting

Nadia into my life, for loving me and then discarding me. I hate—'

'Yes, you said—everything,' he interrupted gently.

He looked down at her and lifted her chin and held it to make sure she didn't escape. His touch was warm and magnetic, his eyes soft as if he understood, and that old weakness surfaced in Jade, nearly making her sway into him again, needing his touch and his comfort and for some sweet words from his lips that would give her hope. She held herself in check, though—it was imperative that she did; already she had shown too much vulnerability. Pride was her saviour at last and she wished she had summoned it before this embarrassing display of weakness in front of him and Nadia.

There was a very small smile on his lips as he added, 'You know, I would have put money on Nadia bursting into tears just now instead of you.'

She stared up at him with shame widening her eyes. Oh, God, she must have come across as some ogre. She hadn't wanted to hurt Nadia; she...she liked her and her idea was good but not quite right, and if Jade hadn't been powered by her own personal trauma she could have got together with her and they perhaps could have come up with something more suitable between them. But she hadn't thought at the time because her heart and the suffering it was being forced to endure had taken precedence.

'It wasn't her fault,' she murmured, lowering her chin out of his grasp. 'I'll apologise to her.' She sniffed and Mel took a handkerchief from his pocket and pressed it into her hand. Jade wiped her face. 'I suppose she laundered this for you,' she couldn't resist saying, and then instantly regretted it because the thought brought more tears to her eyes. She swallowed hard. 'How will she feel washing my lipstick from it?' She held it out to him and he took it and stuffed it back into his pocket.

'Nadia doesn't do my laundry,' he told her gently, and the corners of his mouth crinkled as if the thought amused him.

'Everything else, though,' Jade said wearily. She was getting herself together again and hating what she had done—attacking Nadia like that and then breaking down in front of the pair of them and Mel trying to comfort her as if she was some poor wretch who needed his consolation. But she did need consolation, some sort of help, because she was finding it all so difficult. In another moment of weakness she spoke.

'I can't bear it any more, Mel,' she admitted in a quiet voice. 'I thought I could cope with it all and I can't.'

Then, instantly regretting the weak confession, she put space between them. She stepped back and sank wearily down onto a sofa that had just been delivered that morning. It was still covered in its protective shroud of polythene. She sat on her hands, staring down at the polished oak floor, thinking bleak thoughts. He had organised all this—the new presentation room, the video studio next door, all ready to start in the next few days. He could save the company but at a price—the price of her heart and emotions.

'What exactly is it you can't cope with?' he asked quietly.

He should have known but at times like this he never did. He thought it was all about this power he was wielding within the company, trying out new ideas. And that was a part of it but nothing like the truth. She loved him so much and he had led her to believe they had a second chance but it was all a wicked ruse.

'I can't cope with you and Nadia and everything,' she went on faintly. 'You side with her, against me.'

He came and stood in front of her, lifted her hand and urged her up to her feet.

'How absurd you are. You can't keep your personal life out of your business—'

'It's impossible!' she protested with a sudden surge of strength. 'The whole situation is impossible.'

'It isn't. It's hard but it isn't impossible. If you are suffering because of what you think about me and Nadia then you must have a fair idea about what I've been through in the past.'

'You are going through nothing, Mel! You haven't the sensitivity to suffer.' She knew that wasn't true, knew that he had suffered, but he had put himself through it, made it worse for himself by not listening to her.

He was still holding her wrists, and even in the midst of a row and her own distress she was aware of his strength and his magnetism and knew her need for him would never die. But he had no need. His eyes were as darkly unforgiving as always.

'But you've always tried to win, haven't you?' His voice was suddenly sour with bitterness. 'Wanting it all—'

'Nicholas?' She seethed with frustration at his unreasonable accusation. 'Always Nicholas! And what about Nadia? You throw Nicholas at me and yet you have her, and she is worse because you talk of marriage to her.' She tried to stop her eyes filling with tears again but it was impossible. But what did it matter? She had nothing left to hide from him.

His grip on her tightened. 'I found you betrayed me yet again,' he grazed, his voice like slivers of needle-sharp ice. 'There is no end to it with you, Jade.'

'Because I know I'm wasting my time with explanations,' Jade whispered plaintively. Her tears spilled then, hot and salty, cascading over the rims of her dark eyes and trickling down the side of her nose. 'I never told you about Nicholas four years ago because he wasn't important. You and I...we...we were lovers and...and nothing and no one else mattered. I admit I should have mentioned him and I had every intention of introducing you to him at my party, but because of my father I didn't get the chance.'

'And this time? You had several opportunities to bring Nicholas up,' he reasoned, and Jade thought she detected a softening of his tone and took advantage of it.

'I know,' she murmured, and wiped a tear from her cheek as she lowered her head. 'I don't really have an explanation for that.' She shrugged. 'At first it didn't matter because you were only back in my life on a business footing, and then...' She raised her head and bravely looked into his dark, still suspicious eyes. 'I don't know, Mel; I don't know what was going through my head that night we made love. We were working over supper and I was thinking about our past and how it once was between us and then...' She sighed helplessly. 'I didn't think of Nicholas. He's not often there, just uses the apartment when he's in town. Everything was so good with us and...and he just wasn't important.'

It sounded so feeble, so totally unconvincing, and he wasn't believing her. She drew in a ragged breath. 'I know I've hurt you, Mel; it was never intentional but...but you know, it isn't a lot different for me. You've never met Nicholas and I see Nadia every day. You eventually admitted you had no firm commitment to her and I accepted it. Yet you go off together every night and I don't even know if you live together or not.'

'Maybe you don't care enough to find out,' he suggested darkly.

'Maybe I care so much that I don't want to *know*,' she grazed back at him, hurt to think... Oh, what was the point? He could never forgive her and was only grudgingly listening now.

He said nothing and Jade couldn't even begin to imagine what was going on in his head. And then he took her completely by surprise by lowering his mouth to hers. Her head swam with the intensity of the kiss and confusion ran riot in her very soul. What was this—a test for them both, to see if either of them cared enough to forget their past and get on with the future?

Her eyes narrowed as she pulled back from him, angry and hurt and, as always, confused by his actions. 'What was that—more punishment for me?'

'Who is punishing whom isn't too clear at the moment,' he said harshly. 'Let's take a rain check on revenge for the time being and get back to what we are both here in this building for: business.'

With that he turned on his heel, and was about to sweep out of the room, leaving her standing in the middle of the floor, small and ineffectual, insignificant, in fact, when a last plaintive cry came from her tortured lips, his name echoing in the stillness of the vast room.

He turned and fixed his hard gaze on her, shoulders stiff with pent-up tension as he waited in the doorway to hear what she had to say.

A part of her cried out that it was too late, but the soft, vulnerable side of her urged the words to her pale lips nevertheless.

'J-just one more thing, Mel,' she whispered. 'I never stopped loving you in those four years apart. I never stopped regretting what happened that night. You were my first love, my only love, and the very worst thing of all is that I still love you. I don't want to because it isn't a pleasure to feel this way, but I do love you. I shall have to live with that but...but I just wanted you to know, now, like this, because I know it's all impossible.

There is no hope for us. Hope for my company maybe but nothing for me and you.'

She held his gaze long enough to convince herself that he was not going to allow any reaction to her words to show in the still hard gaze he was bestowing on her. She didn't even regret her heartfelt admission. Perhaps she could draw strength from it, knowing that she had done and said everything that was true to her and there was nothing left inside her that he didn't know about. But for the moment she just felt a deep numbness.

Mel said nothing. Mel showed nothing. No feeling, nothing. He held her gaze for another agonising minute and then he turned away from her and went out the door.

Jade stood for a while, staring blindly at the space where he had been standing. The numbness inside her was good, not bad. She needed it. Slowly she smoothed down her jacket and bravely lifted her chin. She wasn't insignificant after all. In spite of Mel Biaggio she was going to come out of this with her business pride on top, if nothing else.

Determinedly Jade went straight to the studio and made her peace with Nadia. Her apology came out automatically, the words spoken without any thought, but they must have been the right words because Nadia took it well enough for Jade to persuade her that with a few amendments the presentation could be put forward after all. To her credit Nadia was open to Jade's suggestions and together they came up with something that was agreeable to both, keeping in mind Jade's familiarity with Osbourne's and Nadia's flair and originality.

It was only when the session was over that Jade realised what it had cost her. She felt so completely drained that by the time she left Nadia and got to her own office she wasn't fit to speak any more and her legs could hardly carry her inside to pick up her coat and bag and leave.

She didn't tell Diane where she was going and as far as she knew Diane hadn't asked. Of Mel there was no sign.

Back at her apartment she soaked in the bath and read a letter from her father that had been waiting for her when she got in. She was still numb, the world locked out of her mind. Her father's letter was a welcome distraction to lose herself in and so channel her thoughts in another direction. He said he was coming back to the UK next week and would she make sure the house was OK and he had some good news for her but would wait to tell her in person.

Perhaps he was going to marry Anita, she mused. And why not? Anita had mellowed him since they had taken up together three years back. He didn't manipulate her as he manipulated everyone else in his life. Anita was strong-willed and very beautiful and very clever—a match for her father. Jade would be quite happy to see her father married at last but... but how ironic that he should have happiness when a few ill-chosen words from him had ruined his own daughter's happiness. Oh, no, it was all coming back, the pain and the loss. She crumpled her father's letter and flung it across the bathroom.

At that moment the security buzzer went.

'All right, all right!' Jade muttered impatiently, slopping out of the bath and struggling into her old towelling bathrobe.

'Jade? It's Mel. Can I come in?' came the disembodied voice over the intercom.

'Mel?' she breathed. Oh, why couldn't he leave her alone? Had Nadia gone behind her back and complained bitterly about the amendments to the presentation and now he'd come to tear her off another strip?

She opened the apartment door to him, barefoot, warm and damp and feeling at a distinct disadvantage in her worn old robe belted tightly around her tiny waist. Her stomach was tight with tension and she willed her old friend, numbness, to make an appearance.

He strode across the threshold without making any comment and with a deep sigh Jade closed the door after him. He was still dressed in his navy suit so he must have come straight from the office.

She raked her tousled hair from her forehead impatiently. 'What do you want, Mel?'

'Bin bag. Do you possess such a thing?' He wrenched at a cupboard under the sink, nearly pulling it off its hinges. 'Found one!'

Astonished, Jade watched him flick out the bag as he crossed the living area. 'Mel, what the devil are you doing?' she cried.

'Something I should have done a long time ago—exorcising Nicholas Fields from our lives instead of punishing us.' He strode into the spare bedroom, flung open the wardrobe and started stuffing Nicholas's suits and jackets into the bag. Jade stood in the doorway, gazing at him wildly.

'Mel! What the hell are you doing?' she repeated hoarsely.

He swung on her, all dark Mediterranean anger, and his index finger came up, rooting her to the spot. 'If you argue with me I leave, Jade. This is the only way I can deal with this.'

Jade's heart thudded nervously. 'Throwing Nicholas's clothes out? I don't understand. What sort of a way is that, and a way to what? What are you talking about?'

'Our future, our life together,' he told her in clipped tones.

Jade's heart started to race. She was dazed with shock. Their future? This was all to do with their future? Confused, she stepped right into the room. Mel moved to the chest of drawers and pulled them open, stuffing the contents into the bag.

'I've been a fool, Jade. I've allowed my jealousy to spoil it all and this is the only way I can deal with it,' he grated as he worked. 'I've allowed this and this—' he threw ties and socks into the bag '—to twist my reasoning till I'm half-crazed with it.' He stopped suddenly and looked at her stricken features and his whole body seemed to sag.

And suddenly Jade knew what was happening and a great gush of relief flooded her till she felt dizzy with happiness. Now she understood, oh, how she understood, and it was the most wonderful feeling. This was his way—the only way he could come to terms with it all.

'Don't try and stop me, Jade,' he warned as she came and stood beside him, tugging the bag from his hand and letting it drop to the floor.

Jade leaned her head against his shoulder and clung to his arm. 'Oh, I'm not going to stop you, darling,' she murmured. 'I might even help you when I get my breath back.' She smiled, looking up into his drawn face.

Suddenly she was in his arms and they were clinging to each other.

'Can you ever forgive me, darling?' he breathed emotionally into her hair. 'Blame my jealousy, blame anything, but forgive me. I can't live with myself if you don't. It tore at my very soul to hear you opening your heart to me in the studio. You thought you'd lost it all and yet in your pain you couldn't help telling me how much you loved me and always had. I couldn't take it all in, not then. I was so shocked, riddled with guilt, felt such a bastard for what I'd done to you. I had to walk away, get out of your sight because what you'd said had brought home to me just how deeply I had hurt you.'

'Oh, Mel,' she groaned, lifting her flushed face to look at him. 'I told you I couldn't cope any more and—'

'I know, darling, and I can't cope any longer without you. I had to come and rid myself of all that was tormenting me. You living with this Nicholas and—'

She lifted her fingers to his lips, to still the mention of him, and as the tension drained from Mel's face she linked her arms around his neck and tenderly pulled him down to her waiting lips. It was over—the tension, the pain, the exhausting emotional turmoil of loving him and losing him again and again. Mel was with her, wanting a future with her, loving her and wanting her forgiveness. And this was her forgiveness, her kiss of love and tenderness—all that needed to be said in the best way she knew.

He wrapped his arms around her and it was like a vice of sweet possession. His mouth was in her hair, his murmurings incoherent amidst the rush of blood to her head. Then he drew back, lifted her and carried her through to her own room where he deposited her at the foot of the bed. His eyes were dark and predatory as he tugged at the belt of her robe. A small smile tipped the corners of his sensuous mouth.

'What a deplorable robe,' he teased softly.

'It's had its day,' she murmured, lifting her hands to smooth them down the sides of his face.

'It's had its night too.' One last small tug and the belt was free and the robe gaped open, revealing her warm, scented, wanting flesh.

Mel scooped her against him, and rubbed his cheek gently against hers, whispering, 'I'm going to love you for ever, my pocket-sized princess.'

Jade thought her heart would burst with happiness as he lifted her again and set her down on the bed. She knelt up to help him shed his clothes. Her hands smoothed over him, anxious with need, her heart pulsing with love. Her measure of happiness couldn't be excelled, his measure of need was as glorious as ever.

Urgency took precedence, as if they were afraid the outside world would encroach at any time and snatch the moment of bonding passion from them. The rush of kisses and tormented caresses drove them harder and swifter till they were on the brink of ecstasy.

Jade closed around him as he entered her. They were so perfect together, made for each other, and they always had been. He held himself above her, watching her face as he penetrated her so completely that she bit hard on her lower lip. They gazed in wonder at each other, relishing the power of feeling that swept over them as their lower bodies surged against each other... long, silky thrusts, quickening slightly, exquisite shafts of sensuality that fired their whole bodies till the heat nearly engulfed them.

Jade let out small moans of pleasure and moved with him, grasping him to her, squeezing her eyes tight shut because his passion was so incredibly erotic. Higher they rose, out of body, beyond anything that was real. Then came a pulsing, throbbing rush of liquid power and then the ballooning of fluid gold inside, Mel still thrusting inside her, bringing her down and down, hot and floaty, blanketed in love and security.

They lay together, locked in each other's arms, too sated and languid to speak yet. Later they would talk and make promises that never again would they be parted. Mel mouthed kisses against her cheek and ran a warm hand over her burning breasts and Jade wanted the world to end because nothing could ever be better than this.

Jade was the first to hear the small, familiar sound of a key in the lock. Her heart faltered and almost stopped and then she relaxed against the weight of Mel's body. Mel was sleeping peacefully. He had dealt with this, come to terms with his destructive jealousy, and there was nothing to fear now. But this wasn't exactly the right time for him to meet Nicholas and carefully she slid out of bed and slipped on her robe.

She would have to tell Nicholas everything and he would have to leave the apartment, of course. She knew he would understand. He'd probably be horribly mortified that he had inadvertently been the cause of so much trouble.

Nicholas was slumped on the sofa in the living room, eyes closed, looking pale and as exhausted as usual. Jade smiled and ruffled his hair as she passed. Trisha would sort him out once they were married. He worked and travelled far too much.

'I see you're not too tired to have poured yourself a drink.' She smiled down at him.

Nicholas lifted the whisky to his lips and drained the measure. Then he opened his eyes and looked at Jade, who had perched herself on the arm of the sofa next to him.

Perhaps now wasn't exactly the right time to tell him all his clothes were bundled into a bag in his bedroom. Poor Nicholas; he'd never, ever done anything wrong. Mel knew that now and perhaps they could be friends one day. 'What's wrong?' she asked. Nicholas didn't look at all well. He looked as if he'd had a few before the one in his hand.

'I'm sorry, Jade,' he moaned. He reached for her hand and gripped it. 'I wish to hell I'd never suggested him. I blame myself—'

'Mel—Mel Biaggio?' Jade breathed, and then grinned at Nicholas. He'd always been worried about Mel, worried that he'd gone beyond the call of duty with the company for some ulterior motive. 'He's here,' she told him gently. 'Sleeping at the moment.'

'Good God!' Nicholas grated, and tried to get up, but Jade stilled him with one hand.

'It's OK, Nicholas. I've loads to tell you. It's a long story but, well, he's here and—' she sighed happily '—well, he's just here.' Where to begin to explain? she wondered.

Nicholas's eyes flew over her robe and took in the contented flush of her face and in a shock of realisation he shot to his feet, staggering with the force of his own movement as if he'd no control over it. Miraculously, however, he managed to hold onto the crystal-cut glass tumbler containing the remainder of his whisky.

And then Nicholas wasn't gaping at her any more but was looking beyond her, over her shoulder, to the door that led to the inner hallway and the bedrooms. Jade turned, knowing Mel would be standing there. He was. Dressed, shirt open at the neck and tieless. Tall and powerful, seeming twice the height and width of Nicholas in his charcoal-grey suit.

Jade would rather their first meeting had been on more neutral ground but she hadn't known Nicholas was going to be in town this evening and of course she hadn't known Mel was coming round... Anyway it had happened. She opened her mouth to hurry out the introductions, acutely aware that the two men were eyeing each other warily, Nicholas slightly the worse for drink and Mel somewhat pale yet with a steely determination about him that suggested to Jade he was controlling his feelings and trying to come to terms with meeting the source of his past jealousy.

'Mel, this is—'

She didn't finish. There was a muted roar from...from Nicholas? In disbelief Jade watched as Nicholas lurched forward towards Mel, the movement, to Jade's frenzied wide eyes, seeming to happen in slow motion. Nicholas, wild with fury, lurching at Mel.

'You bastard! You thieving bastard!'

His fist came back and Jade shrieked in alarm and flew across the room. Mel stood his ground, so coldly impassive that Jade wondered if he knew what was happening. Nicholas was going to punch him! It was impossible. Surely if any punches were going to be landed Mel was the one to have cause to throw them?

Nicholas punched the air as, with only the slightest of movements, Mel avoided the blow. The impact of Nicholas's fist on the yielding air couldn't have shocked him more if it had landed on Mel's unyielding jawline. He lurched, stumbled, nearly overbalanced completely, and would have done if Mel hadn't hauled him up by his collar. He swung him around and with one powerful hand pinned him against the wall next to the microwave, his other hand clenched in readiness to defend himself should Nicholas chance another punch at him.

'What the hell do you think you're doing?' he grated roughly, almost shaking Nicholas to tumble a reason from his white lips.

'Leave him, Mel,' Jade said quickly. Poor Nicholas looked as if he was going to choke.

'I'll leave him when he tells me what this is about.'

'As if you didn't bloody know,' Nicholas grazed.

'Nicholas, what's wrong?' Jade pleaded. She hadn't a clue what was going on here. Why on earth was Nicholas so mad with Mel?

Nicholas glared at Mel with fury but directed his words at Jade. 'He hasn't told you, has he?'

'Told me what?' Jade asked in amazement. These two didn't know each other and yet it was she who was feeling out of it, as if she wasn't a part of what was going on.

Suddenly Mel let Nicholas go and Nicholas sagged against the wall. He was still defying Mel with his eyes as he straightened his tie at his throat and then somewhat nervously smoothed his hands down his suit jacket.

Mel stood impassive before him, his threatening presence enough to quell any more fury that might have erupted from Nicholas. He didn't speak a word and somehow his ominous silence caused fear to stab at Jade's spine.

'Please, what is it?' she murmured nervously. Instinctively she felt that Mel knew what Nicholas was on about. 'Tell me if it concerns me,' she insisted. What was happening here?

'You can't tell her, can you?' Nicholas challenged Mel, and Jade wondered if she was invisible. 'You rotten, cheap, lousy—'

Mel's hand shot out to grip his tie threateningly, his eyes dark with fury. He held onto Nicholas, the grip on him so debilitating that Nicholas couldn't have uttered another insult if his life had depended on it.

'That's enough from you,' Mel breathed heavily, obviously winning the battle to hold onto his temper, but only just. Jade had never seen his face so white and taut. 'If it comes from anyone it'll come from me. I don't want to know where you got your information from because I've got a good idea. There are only two people in the world who know, and since this is the first time

we've met it can only have come from John
Ritchie.'

'Mel!' Jade cried, her heart thudding which shock at
the mention of her father. 'Mel, what on earth...?' Real
fear spiralled through her now. Oh, God, what had
happened?

Mel let Nicholas go and turned to her then. That cold
hostility didn't soften for her and her heart was twisting
in agony now, the fear getting a deeper hold, paling her
skin, thinning her blood till she felt faint. Mel spoke
quietly, almost formally, without warmth or tenderness.
'I would have told you when I thought the time was right.
Now isn't exactly the time but I don't want it coming
from him.' He nodded towards a white-faced Nicholas
who looked as if he wished he could go out and come
back in again.

'I did a deal with your father last week,' he told Jade
levelly. 'He's coming back to the UK next week to tell
you himself. He sold me Ritchie's—'

Jade's hands shot to her mouth in shock and her eyes
widened painfully. Oh, no this couldn't be true. This
couldn't have happened without her knowledge. It just
couldn't.

'And the rest, you bastard,' Nicholas suddenly grated,
brave all of a sudden.

There was more? What more could there be? Mel
owned the company—the company her father had trusted
her to run for the past four years. She had always thought
it would all come to her eventually...and now it was
Mel's and...

'Jade,' Mel murmured, his tone warning her that 'the
rest' Nicholas had mentioned was something she wasn't
going to enjoy hearing. 'I'm giving the company
to...to Nadia.'

The words, the name, the meaning slammed into her as if Nicholas's fist had landed in the pit of her stomach instead of punching at thin air. But Mel had delivered the verbal blow and the breath went from her. Winded, she tried to gasp out, No, no, but nothing came to her whitened lips. Her head spun dizzily and she clenched her fists to try and keep herself from collapsing, and then realisation seeped through the fog in her mind.

She stared in horror at Mel. Mel who had come to her tonight, begging forgiveness, putting right all that he'd allowed to go wrong. Loving her, making love to her... knowing all this. He had planned and plotted all this way back, from the very start. It wasn't Jade and Mel, it was Nadia and Mel. It always had been.

His words of love had meant nothing; his lovemaking had been a charade to fool her into a false sense of security so that subsequently, when she was at her most defenceless, he could snatch it all away from her, punish her, destroy her. Suddenly she knew so much, realised so much. Pain? The pain of the past had been nothing to what she felt now. It was as if he had torn her very heart out and discarded it, shredded and useless.

A deep, numbing chill clawed her from head to toe. Mel had won. Four years ago her supposed betrayal had damaged him so badly it had turned him into the monster of revenge he was now. And he was a monster—a terrible, evil man—and it helped to know it now. He had destroyed her love, stamped it underfoot as if it had no worth.

The iron bars of protection came up around her heart; she willed them up, and bolted them firmly against him.

Jade breathed deeply and drew herself up. Stiffly she walked away from the two of them, cold, oh, so cold, thinking that even if they killed each other she couldn't care less.

CHAPTER NINE

'MEL rang to say he'll be a bit late,' Diane told her the next morning as she crossed the outer office and went into her own. 'Are you OK, Jade?' she asked worriedly.

'Fine,' Jade told her from the door, forcing a thin smile. She wasn't, of course. She still felt horribly disorientated after her shocking discovery but she had to keep going, for the staff's sake, if nothing else.

'Mel didn't sound fine; he sounded—'

Like a bastard, Jade didn't add, closing her door after her. She sat down at her desk and gazed around her, her face pinched with lack of sleep. This wasn't hers any more, not even her father's. She had nothing—no career, no life. Tears stung her eyes but she wouldn't allow herself the luxury of a good old weep. She'd survive because she'd survived four years without him and she was getting the hang of it. Mel had taught her one thing, though—that when you were down the only way out was up—but where she was going to ascend to was anyone's guess.

'Can you spare a minute, Jade?' a voice came from the door.

Jade looked up from the desk drawer she was numbly clearing, surprised to see Nadia hovering in the doorway. She wouldn't be able to bear it if Nadia had come to thank her for the company Mel had bought for her. That would be the final agony, the one that would send her over the edge.

'I just came to thank you...' she began as she crossed the room to Jade, and Jade's heart slumped to an all-

162

time low. Somehow she braced herself in defence. 'Your
input into the Osbourne presentation was invaluable,
Jade. I can see now that I'd gone way over the top. Even
Mel hadn't seen it. I didn't tell him about the alterations
you suggested and went ahead and sent a courier over
last night with the artwork. They accepted it first thing
this morning, jubilantly, and they wouldn't have done
if I'd stuck to my guns and not listened to you.' Her
eyes twinkled suddenly. 'I think we make a good team,
don't you?'

Jade stared at her bleakly, wondering if Nadia was
quite as innocent as she seemed. But perhaps she didn't
know that she now owned Ritchie's. Maybe it was going
to be a little engagement surprise from Mel!

Oh, the pain and the anguish of it all. She forced words
to her thinned lips. 'I'm glad it worked out,' was all she
could form in a faint whisper.

Nadia grinned happily and leaned across Jade's desk,
an elongated string of jet beads swinging from her lovely
pale throat. She stilled them with her long, artistic
fingers. 'Who's going to tell him, you or me?' she teased
lightly.

She has his measure, Jade thought with a dull thud
of her heart. She knows him so well. Yet looking at her,
arty and bohemian, Jade felt she wasn't his type. But
then they said that opposites attracted. What did Jade
know anyway? Apparently nothing where Mel Biaggio
was concerned.

She shook her head because there was no answer to
Nadia's query. She wouldn't be here anyway, to tell
anyone anything. She was out of it all and any minute
now she was going to get up and walk out and leave the
two of them to it.

Nadia plopped herself down in the chair on the other
side of Jade's desk and suddenly she wasn't teasing and

twinkling any more. Her lovely face had taken on a new seriousness.

'Jade, I also want to thank you for giving me this chance. I don't know how much Mel has told you, but, knowing him, not a lot. I adore him, Jade. He gives so much of himself...'

Oh, dear God, please stop, Jade wanted to plead. I don't want to hear. Not girl talk, not now. It's unendurable. But there was no stopping Nadia.

'I've been to hell and back and for the first time I'm feeling as if I've got a grasp on life again, thanks to you—and Mel, of course.' She sighed softly. 'It was so hard for me when I found I was pregnant and...Mel was so strong, and then after I lost the baby...'

Nausea rose up in Jade's throat, hot and stinging. Nadia pregnant with Mel's baby? Oh, no, please, no. Enough was enough. She couldn't take any more.

'Mel's stood by me and—'

Jade's strength came back in a feverish rush. Her head swimming with pain, she forced movement to her legs. Grabbing her handbag with trembling fingers, she flew from the room, ignoring Nadia's cry of concern for her.

Mel caught her arm in the outer office and she was so dazed with grief she didn't know what was happening.

'This isn't the time to be leaving, Jade,' he said gently. 'We have things to talk about.'

Jade's head reeled; her first coherent thought was that he hadn't shouted at her and ordered her back into her office. Gradually her head cleared, her eyes focused, and her whole body stiffened. He stood towering over her, grasping her arm with one hand, holding a huge bunch of deep red roses in the other. Nadia stood bemused in the doorway, Diane sat bemused at her desk, and all the phones seemed to be ringing at the same time. Jade saw

a red mist before her eyes, a billowing mist of fierce
rage.

'You rat!' she breathed in fury. 'How dare you humiliate me this way? How dare you?' How could he be
so cruel? What was buried in the heart of those roses
for Nadia—her company deeds, bound with red ribbon
to match the blooms? She couldn't bear it; it was way
over the top, too much to face. 'I hate you for this! I
hate myself for allowing it to happen!' she screamed at
him. 'I never want to see you again, ever!' And she fled,
with Mel's voice calling her name ringing in her ears.

The air outside, fresh wintry air blustering in from the
west, cooled her temples but did nothing to cool the heat
inside her. She burned with it. Mel and Nadia had created
a child and it hurt so terribly to think about
it...and...and they had lost it. Poor Nadia. Mel had
stood by her and so he damn well should have, but what
he shouldn't have done was seduce her, Jade, back into
his life when he'd had a commitment to Nadia all along.
Oh, how he had fooled her, and fooled poor Nadia too,
because she couldn't know what Mel was really like.

Nicholas was brewing coffee when Jade, frazzled and
still hot with fury, got back to the apartment later. She
hadn't seen him since the skirmish last night with Mel.
She'd flown to her bedroom and slammed the door shut
after casting Mel's suit jacket out into the hallway so
that she wouldn't have to see him again. And she didn't
want to see Nicholas now either. She wanted her own
space, time to get her head together over this wicked,
cruel betrayal. But seeing as he was here...

'Did you know through my father, Nicholas?' she
shrieked at him. 'Have you spoken to him? What did
he say?'

Nicholas held his hands up in mock surrender. 'Hold
on, Jade. Cool down.'

'I'll never be cool again!' she stormed at him, flinging her bag down on a stool. 'Tell me how you knew.'

Nicholas calmly poured her a coffee and pushed it over the work surface to her. 'He called me at the office yesterday—lucky to find me there actually. As you know, we talk once a month or so.'

Jade kneaded her aching brow. Of course, Nicholas looked after her father's shares portfolio.

'We went through the usual and then he told me about the sale of Ritchie's and where the money was to go. Most of it's to go to you in investments for your future. He said it was time you were married and giving him grandchildren—'

'Planning to marry me off to you again, no doubt,' she flamed. How could her father do this to her? She was mad at him, but her fury with Mel took precedence. It boiled like an inferno inside her.

'Look, I don't pretend to know what is going on here' Nicholas went on wearily. 'You'll tell me in your own good time but for the moment I've got a blinding headache and can well do without you screaming at me.' He swallowed a couple of aspirins with his coffee and it gave Jade time to reason with herself that this wasn't Nicholas's fault.

She clenched her fists. 'Go on,' she urged, calmer now but only marginally so.

'Then he went on to tell me who was taking over. Said this Mel Biaggio had got in touch with him with an offer he couldn't refuse. You could have knocked me down with the back page of the *Financial Times*.' Nicholas gulped more coffee and went on, 'He went on to say what a great guy Biaggio was and how he wouldn't mind him for a son-in-law. God, the bastard even fooled your father. John would have a fit if he knew Nadia was in fact Biaggio's fiancée. I'm beginning to wonder if there's a law against this. I'd call what he did malpractice—worming his fiancée into your company and then snaffling it for her.'

'Unethical, yes,' Jade agreed tightly, reaching for her coffee and wondering if a couple of aspirins or six would lull her into a sleep she didn't want to wake from. 'So my father knew Mel was giving the company to Nadia?'

'Biaggio told him he wanted the shares in her name; said it was to be a gift to her—he omitted to tell him his marriage plans, though.' Nicholas snorted in disgust. 'John was thrilled the company was going to someone so respected in the business. He'd heard of her. Apparently she's very talented, innovative and—'

'Shut up!' Jade cried. The lovely Nadia was a wonderwoman and she didn't need the fact rammed down her throat again and again.

'I could kick myself for letting this happen, Jade,' Nicholas moaned, looking at her and noting the paleness of her face, the grim set of her lips.

'It isn't your fault,' Jade conceded dully.

'Yes, but I had my suspicions, didn't I? I should have acted on them.'

'Yes, well, you did leave it a trifle late to try and land one on him,' she bit back.

He grinned sheepishly. 'I would have done, too, if I hadn't had one over the eight sherbets last night.'

He wouldn't have stood a chance, Jade thought. 'Did he say anything after I left?' she asked after a minute of morbid reflection.

Stupid question really; what did it matter and what difference would it make knowing if he had said anything after she had flounced off last night? Safe behind the locked door of her bedroom, she'd heard no further sounds. She had never thought of either of them as violent and Nicholas's attack had shocked her, but Mel's

cool control had astonished her even more. Hadn't he
always said he'd want to punch the jaw of any man involved with her? Yet he'd restrained himself last night,
hadn't lashed back even when threatened.

With hindsight, it was easy to reason why. He didn't
care about her any more, hadn't cared for four years.
All that love talk and action had just been a ruse to
punish her for denting his pride four years ago, and he'd
added a dollop of crushing revenge by taking the
company from her as well. If Oscars for towering per-
formances in the revenge category were being dished out,
Mel Biaggio would get the prize for best perpetrator, she
decided grimly.

'Actually, he said rather a strange thing,' Nicholas
went on, frowning. 'He went into the hall to pick up his
jacket after you'd tossed it out of your bedroom and
came back and said, "Now I've finally met you I'm
wondering why I tortured myself for so long." That was
all. And then he stormed out. Blowed if I can work that
one out.' Nicholas noticed the expression of despair on
her face. 'Jade, sweetheart,' he said softly. 'I don't mean
to pry but, well, last night you and him—I mean...it
looked...'

'Forget it,' Jade suddenly blazed. 'I don't want to talk
about it. It was nothing; it never has been anything.' She
grabbed her handbag and rushed to her bedroom. She
couldn't bear it. She shouldn't have asked. He'd wondered what he'd tortured himself with over the years!
Huh, he didn't know anything about torture, only how
to inflict it on others.

She packed a few things, quickly and jerkily, trying
not to think. She didn't want to be in town. She needed
air and lots of it. 'I'm going down to Bankton House
for the weekend,' she told Nicholas, noticing he was
leaning in her doorway gripping a steadying cup of coffee

in both hands. 'If Daddy's coming over I'll need to straighten the house out.'

Yes, getting the house ready for her father would give her reason to live. In his letter he'd said he had news for her. God, what a romantic fool she had been to think the news was his engagement to Anita. She knew the news now. Mel Biaggio had bought the company for the real love of his life.

'I don't think you're in a fit state to drive anywhere at the moment, Jade,' Nicholas said sagely. 'I've never seen you so wound up. Why don't we all go down together in the morning? Trisha and I are at a loose end this weekend and—'

'I'm going now!' Jade slammed at him, and grabbed her overnight bag.

Nicholas caught her arm as she went to push past him. 'Jade, go if you must, but we'll come down Sunday. I think you need to talk and we've known each other long enough for you to open up to me.'

A protest hovered on Jade's lips, but not for long. She saw the concern in Nicholas's eyes. At least someone cared about her. Being alone this weekend would mean having no control over her thinking. At least if she was occupied with Nicholas and Trisha, cooking and clearing up after the pair of them, thinking wouldn't be forced on her.

'Suit yourself,' she muttered, and then bit her lip as tears welled in her eyes. She added humbly, 'Thanks, Nicholas. I think you must be the only friend I have in the world.'

The phone started to ring and Jade was glad of the diversion. As Nicholas turned away to answer it, she took the chance to slip away before she broke down altogether.

*   *   *

Jade slammed on the brakes hard. She'd been so deep in miserable thoughts, she was almost on top of the crash before it registered. Ahead a lorry had jackknifed across three lanes of the motorway. Several cars had slammed into it. There was chaos—police lights flashing, a fire crew already hard at work, ambulances and paramedics standing by. One of the cars, its bonnet crumpled under the belly of the articulated lorry, was the same make and colour as her own. Oh, God. It was almost like a sign of what might have happened to her if she hadn't pulled up in time.

Jade shivered, her head clearing. There must have been warning signs way back on the motorway but she just hadn't seen them.

'Keep to the hard shoulder,' a voice shouted, and someone tapped on her window. Instinctively Jade buzzed the window down to the policeman who was directing the traffic. 'The slip road ahead is closed for the rescue teams so keep going down the motorway. Now keep moving before you cause another sticky pile-up.'

Without needing to be told twice Jade cautiously shifted forward, hardly daring to glance at the mass of wreckage to her right. It sobered her thinking. She hadn't been concentrating and Nicholas was right. She shouldn't be driving down to Bankton, not so soon after her own personal shock.

By the time she got home she'd realised just how fragile she was feeling. She was exhausted, mentally and physically. The sun was going down. The house glowed, the stonework mellowed down to an orangey hue. It was one small comfort to her senses. She was home and she'd lock herself away and nothing, but nothing would get to her.

She stood in the hallway for a minute, breathing deeply, and then everything did get to her. For four years, every time she'd entered this house she'd seen that heart-rending image of Mel standing by the buffet bar in the drawing room, ashen-faced with shock after her father's announcement. Misty-eyed, Jade let her eyes wander to the stairs. Now, without even going upstairs she knew the spectre of him would be there, standing by the fire-place in her bedroom, naked, wanting her but acting the honourable gentleman and not taking her.

'Hypocrite!' she ground out between her teeth as she headed determinedly for the kitchen. And clever too. Softly, softly he had seduced her, for punishment and to blind her with love so that she was so befuddled she wouldn't realise he was taking the company away from her. And it had all started out with him kissing her be-cause he supposedly wanted to lay a ghost, to exorcise her from his past. He'd done that right enough and now she was the one with the ghosts and spectres in her head.

She switched on the central heating and busied herself with lighting a fire in the drawing room, trying not to think as she worked. Most of the time she felt dead inside, numb, as if she had no feelings left, and then suddenly the pain would well up inside her and nearly overwhelm her with the misery it caused.

She made coffee, a huge pot of it, and took it through to the drawing room, where she coiled up on the sofa in front of the fire. And then the tears came, hot and painful and very much unbidden.

'Oh, no,' she sobbed into a tissue as she heard a car on the drive. Nicholas and Trisha must have decided to follow her down. She didn't want them yet—not yet.

There was no escape. Every damned light downstairs blazed. Jade got to her feet, scrubbed at her face and sniffed away the last tear.

A gasp of shock broke in the back of her throat and her legs nearly folded beneath her as she opened the front door to Mel. Was he real or just another hallucination in this house of spectres?

Her first instinct was to slam the door in his face but his foot was already in it, as always a step ahead of her! She stared in disbelief at the red roses he held in his arms, a little worse for wear now. Then her eyes shifted to his face and she gasped at the sight of his drawn features.

'Thank God you're safe,' he breathed raggedly, tossing the roses down on the hall table. He stepped towards her as if to gather her in his arms but Jade quickly stepped back out of his reach. The rat! He had the audacity to think she might have harmed herself because of him! Had he expected to find her with her head in the oven or something?

He stood in front of her, not making another attempt to grasp her. He looked so pale and gaunt, and for a second or two Jade wondered if he had a conscience after all and had come to try and make amends.

Before she could unleash her fury on him he spoke.

'When I called you Nicholas told me you were driving down. Said you'd just left and you were in a state. I nearly went crazy when I saw the pile-up on the motorway. A car like yours, crushed under—'

Jade let out a cry of disbelief. 'Huh, you thought it was me, did you?' she cried almost hysterically. 'Perhaps your fat ego led you to believe I'd done it deliberately. Tried to end it all after your wicked rejection. My God, you—'

He gripped her shoulders suddenly, so swiftly that she hadn't a chance to take evasive action. He almost shook her.

'Stop it, Jade. Don't talk that way. You *are* in a state—distraught, not thinking,' he ground out.

Furiously Jade wrenched herself out of his grip. 'I am distraught,' she admitted wildly. 'But I am thinking, Mel—oh, yes, I am. Let's start with those, shall we?' A toss of her head indicated the roses lying on the table. 'Worth second-hand roses, am I? Is Nadia allergic to them or something?'

'They were never intended for Nadia in the first place,' he told her through tight lips. 'They were for you. They *are* for you.'

'My consolation prize?' she bit out, the fury in her eyes defying him to come any closer. 'She gets the company and... and everything and I get the booby prize? Oh, to hell with you. I don't want you here, in my father's home. Get out! You can't have anything to say to me that will be any excuse.'

He faced her fury with equal determination, eyes black now. 'Well, I didn't exactly expect you to greet me with open arms but I did expect you to exhibit a modicum of intelligence and give me room to explain.'

'I don't want your excuses.'

'You won't get any. I said explain, not excuse. Trouble with your hearing as well as your sanity, Jade?' he mocked, and then he gave her a look that could only be interpreted as pitiful and turned his back on her to walk through to the drawing room.

Jade followed him and stopped in the doorway, transfixed by the real-life image of him standing where he had stood years ago, by the drinks table, now helping himself to her father's brandy.

The furious protest on Jade's lips was stilled by the excruciating thought that Mel might have gone all the way—not only bought Ritchie's but this house and its contents and her father's brandy as well!

Mel came to her and handed her a brandy. 'Nothing is what it seems,' he murmured.

She took the glass and glared at him with contempt. 'The beginning of the excuses? I can't wait for you to get to the meaty parts. I mean, what excuse can there be for all the lies and deception you've fooled me with?'

'I've never lied to you and I've never deceived you,' he told her quietly. 'Whatever I have done has always been with your best interests at heart.'

She shook her head and actually laughed at that. He was something else. He ought to be in politics! She supposed she ought to hear him out, and then she would *throw* him out because nothing he would say would make her change her mind about him.

Jade slumped down on the sofa and cradled the brandy glass in her hands. They weren't even shaking. Perhaps she wasn't even here. Perhaps she had died and come back as a hologram!

'Have you heard from your father?' he asked.

Her eyes narrowed dangerously. 'I resent that, you know,' she told him tightly. 'I resent you even mentioning my father, drinking his brandy, in his house...no, don't tell me, it's your house now. You made him an offer he couldn't refuse, you...you Godfather!'

'Grow up, Jade, will you?' he said harshly. 'All I've bought is your father's company, not his life.' He sat in her father's wing chair by the fireside and stared into his brandy glass.

'And what about *my* life? You've sold me down the river,' Jade uttered miserably. 'Hadn't you done enough, Mel—deceiving me with Nadia? But it wasn't enough revenge for you, was it? You wanted a whole lot more— my life's work.' She stood up then and started to pace the hearth. She couldn't keep still. Anger and distrust still burned inside her. 'And you couldn't even tell me about it. I had to hear it from Nicholas. How damned ironic after all these years. You couldn't have stage-managed that better if you'd trained for it. Or perhaps you did...perhaps in those four years out of my life you took a course at the school of irony and deception and—'

'Stop it, Jade!' he ordered, getting to his feet and coming towards her. Jade stopped mid-pace and stared at him. 'You are going way over the top and Nicholas didn't tell you anyway; I did.'

'Because your back was against the wall—'

'Nicholas's was actually,' he joked, and had the audacity to offer her a smile.

'That's not funny,' Jade hissed. 'And you wouldn't have told me if Nicholas hadn't found out.'

He shrugged. 'How do you know I wouldn't have told you?'

Oh, it was a really stupid question. How did she know? Of course she knew. But...

'Well, perhaps you were biding your time.' A thought suddenly struck her and her dark eyes narrowed and her lips thinned. 'Or perhaps you wanted to tell Nadia first—a romantic engagement surprise. "Here you are, darling; something for you to while away the hours with—a little ad agency I picked up on my travels."'

Jade crossed the room and refilled her brandy glass. Suddenly it was snatched out of her hands, she was swung round to face him and she felt sure he would be angry, but though he held her firmly it was without malice. Even the shade of his eyes came as an unexpected surprise; they were a soft grey, like morning mist on the forest floor. Jade felt her silly bones start to melt.

'I want you sober tonight, Jade,' he said tenderly, 'though you're talking so incoherently at the moment I'm beginning to wonder if you're a secret tippler.'

Surely this wasn't a time to joke? A sort of defeat washed through her, sapping the last of her energy. This sudden tenderness wasn't fair.

'Why, Mel?' she whispered, her eyes wide with grief, her white lips trembling the words. 'Why are you here? Don't you think you've put me through enough?' More than enough, she thought. She was teetering on the brink of insanity and just one little push...

His dark, brooding eyes softened. 'That's nothing to what I'm going to put you through in the future, Jade— all pleasurable, I promise you. I would have told you about the agency but your father wanted to tell you. He said it was his duty, not mine. You would have known next week.'

'And when would Nadia have known—tonight, to-morrow, over some candlelit dinner along with soft music and a diamond ring glinting in the heart of... of those red roses you claim you bought for me?'

She pushed at him then, the whole scenario she had conjured up in her mind sickening her to the very core of her being. She moved out of his air space and took up a stance by the fire, leaning one hand on the marble mantel and staring into the glowing coals.

'All for Nadia,' she muttered miserably. 'She gets it all.'

He came and stood behind her. She felt his presence, the heat of him so close to her. His hand smoothed over her shoulder in a comforting gesture and though she resented it she did nothing to stop it.

'She gets very little, darling. Just a new chance at life— and that is very little compared to what she has lost.'

Jade turned her head to him and widened her misty eyes, remembering the loss of their baby. But how could she sympathise? Nadia was getting a second chance and that was more than Mel had offered her.

'I'm...I'm sorry about the baby,' she murmured, and lowered her eyes away from his. She didn't want to see his pain; it would tip her over the edge.

His hand on her shoulder stilled. 'How did you know about the baby?'

Jade stared fixedly into the fire. She didn't want to talk about it; it hurt so much. She licked her dry lips.

'She...Nadia...mentioned it this...this morning.'

He let out a small sigh. 'I'm glad—glad she's got around to talking about it. It's been very painful for her.'

In agony Jade looked up at him again, her fingers clawing into a fist on the mantelpiece.

'Painful for her,' she husked. 'Yes, it must have been.' Her eyes suddenly brimmed with hot tears. 'And you're glad she's got around to talking about it, are you?' She couldn't help the derision in her tone. She stepped back from him, knocking his hand from her shoulder with force. Her eyes blazed with the fierceness of her tears. 'And how do you think I felt listening to that, Mel, knowing you had such a deep relationship with her you had made a baby together? I never had that chance. You slammed out of my life four years ago, not giving me the chance to make babies with you!'

Mel looked incredulous at her outburst and then suddenly he took her tenderly by the shoulders again. His eyes softened and for a second Jade thought she saw a smirk—or was it a smile?—lurking at the corners of his lips.

'Jade, darling, you haven't been torturing yourself—?'

Jade wriggled furiously out of his grasp and stepped back from him, eyes shining with anger. Oh, it was a smirk, and he was going to ridicule her now and she just couldn't take it.

'No, *you* are the master of torture!' she cried. 'I suppose you have some very plausible excuse—'

'I've never made a baby with Nadia,' he told her earnestly. 'I've never even slept with Nadia.'

Jade opened her mouth to make a vicious retort, but something stopped her from uttering it. It...it was such a preposterous denial...it...it could be true.

'Mel?' she croaked.

He stepped forward and cupped her face in his strong, warm hands and his eyes were deep with emotion as he spoke. 'Darling, you're mistaken. I don't know what Nadia told you but obviously it wasn't everything, and I know that she thinks so highly of you she wouldn't purposely lead you to believe her pregnancy was anything to do with me.'

Jade opened her mouth and a small croak came out. She swallowed hard. 'I...I don't understand.'

Mel lowered his mouth to hers and caught her trembling lips in a kiss so warm and loving and caring that she felt that little loop of hope do a skip in her heart. Mel was here, had arrived fraught with distress after thinking she had been involved in that pile-up, and now he was denying he was the father of Nadia's lost baby and...and he was kissing her so beautifully, so deeply, as if he would never let her out of his life again.

He drew back from her, his eyes eating her up, his hands smoothing down the sides of her face. 'It's you I love, Jade,' he told her with deep feeling. 'It always has been you and always will be you.'

Oh, she wanted to believe him, so very much, but there was so much evidence against it.

'Mel,' she whispered plaintively. 'You can't love me and do the things you do. To take my company and—'

'That first meeting with you, I was so mad, still hurt, still bleeding inside and wanting to hurt you. I thought you were married and then when you said you weren't the hope began to burn. I knew I wanted you back in my life, completely—no half-measures.'

Jade's head swam. 'But the company—'

'Own your company, own you. I couldn't bear the thought of getting Ritchie's back on its feet and then just walking away from it and you. Fate had brought us together again; it was another chance for us both.'

'But...but you had Nadia. You didn't want me. Here, in this house, when I was ill, you...you wouldn't...'

'Because you were ill and had been delirious and I couldn't be sure if it was the real you or not. And I did have Nadia but—'

'There can't be any buts, Mel,' Jade appealed. 'You'd said you were engaged; you were committed to Nadia, and then you brought her into the company and now...now you've bought it for her and...and I don't understand,' she finished feebly.

Mel let his hands drop to his sides. It was then that Jade felt her knees go weak. He looked so solemn it frightened her. She sank down to the sofa and he sat with her, leaning his elbows on his knees as he gazed into the fire.

'I've known Nadia for a few years now,' Mel told her. 'We met through mutual friends. She was engaged to be married at the time...'

Jade gulped, clenching her hands in her lap. Nadia engaged to someone else? She had been close in once thinking she might be married. Had Mel broken up that engagement?

'She was at the peak of her career and had just won a major award for an advertising campaign. She had everything to live for and then discovered she was pregnant. She was over the moon.' Mel paused.

'And she lost it,' Jade finished for him, her voice small and wavery with sympathy for Nadia.

'Carl, her lover, wanted her to have an abortion.'

Jade gasped and bit her lower lip. Surely Nadia hadn't agreed? She wasn't the sort. She was a sweet, caring person.

'Nadia took it badly. She wanted the child. She couldn't believe the man she loved didn't feel the same way. It was then that she started to go to pieces. The relationship broken down and her work suffered. She wouldn't agree to an abortion and Carl walked out on her. Two weeks later, four months pregnant, she lost the baby. A month after that she tried to commit suicide.'

'Oh, no!' Jade cried, her heart hammering so hard she felt faint. Oh, no, poor Nadia. How desperate she must have felt to go to those lengths. Dizzily Jade spun her thoughts back to when she had lost Mel. Though she had been desperate she didn't think taking her own life had been a serious thought. To actually attempt it...

'She must have loved him very much,' Jade breathed sadly.

Mel shook his head. 'He wasn't the absolute cause of her breakdown, although now she hates him, of course. It was a combination of things, although losing the baby was at the root of it all. She blamed herself, saw it as some sort of perverse punishment for picking the wrong man. She couldn't get her career back on course and that hit her badly. She just lost control of her life and death seemed the only option. She took an overdose. She was staying in one of my apartments at the time—'

'Regent's Park?' Jade asked softly.

He nodded and raised his dark eyes to meet hers. 'I told you I'd taken on the rest of the property.'

'For... for a family.'

He half smiled. 'A crazy hope that you would come back into my life one day and we'd live happily ever after.'

Jade lowered her lashes. So the same hope had lain in his heart too.

'You . . . you found Nadia?'

He nodded. 'I rushed her to hospital and I've looked after her ever since.' He let out a ragged sigh. 'You'd be amazed at the way friends slide out of the scene when a breakdown occurs. She was so unstable, people didn't want to know.'

'That's what you meant when you said she was grateful, and it explains why, that first day I met her, when she started to thank me for giving her the opportunity, you whisked me away.' Oh, she understood now; she hadn't had an inkling before that anything so tragic had happened to Nadia.

Mel nodded. 'I didn't want you or anyone else to know what she had been through in case it affected the way you treated her. She was so afraid of people's reactions, had such a low self-esteem that she was barely able to function. Joining Ritchie's was a new start for her—new people to work with, none of them knowing what she had been through. I'm glad she opened up to you. It shows she trusts you and has the confidence in herself now to talk to you about it.'

'Oh, Mel,' Jade moaned. 'I didn't listen, not properly. I just blundered out, not wanting to hear about your . . . what I thought was your baby.' Suddenly Jade reached out and covered his hand with her own, feeling so guilty for everything she had thought. 'And, Mel, you bought the company for her and not to hurt me.'

He lifted her chin and kissed her lips lightly but warmly. 'I've hurt you enough in the past, my darling. Initially I wanted the company as a means of laying a claim to you. The thought of giving it to Nadia came later. She's done so well and she loves the work and her life is back on track once more. I considered a partnership, you and her, but the more I thought of it, the more I knew I didn't want to share you, even with Nadia. At this moment in time you need me more than she does.' His eyes softened. 'Nadia is doing fine. I suspect she might be seeing Dave Rand on a more personal basis before very long.'

Jade's eyes widened. How had she missed that? Quite easily, she supposed. When you were in love yourself other loves didn't interest you.

'I wanted to give her something special, a new start; surely you can understand that?'

Her head was swimming with happiness but she managed a nod. Yes, she understood, and loved him for caring for Nadia.

'And I wanted you entirely free to devote your life to me,' he added with a sudden gleam in his eye.

Jade let out a small, soft laugh to cover the racing of her heartbeat. 'Oh, Mel Biaggio, that is fighting talk.'

'Well, let it be the last fight we ever have.'

Jade shook her head, her eyes suddenly gleaming too. 'I can't promise that, Mel,' she teased softly.

He grazed a tempting kiss across her mouth and then gathered her into his arms, and she clung to him, arms around his neck, holding him tight, as if to show that he would never escape her again. 'I can promise that I'll love you for ever, though,' she told him passionately.

'You'll have to when you marry me,' he growled in her ear.

She looked at him and smiled happily, all her worries easing away, her heart lifting, all the terrible anguish gone for ever. 'Is that a real live marriage proposal?' she asked.

'Absolutely. And the last, because I won't take no for an answer.'

Jade frowned teasingly. 'But can I trust you? Were you really considering marrying Nadia? You led me to believe you were.'

'I was talking through my pain—wanting you so much and yet unable to forget that awful moment in my life when I heard you were engaged to be married. It scarred me so badly. I went crazy after that, and I might have been crazy enough to ask Nadia to marry me if you hadn't asked for my professional services. But it would have been a loveless marriage—for both of us. Nadia and I are fond of each other but—'

'Like Nicholas and me,' Jade murmured, her eyes searching his. Had he really forgiven her or was he just storing his anger away to be dredged up at some time of weakness?

Mel sighed. 'You know, my relationship with Nadia is similar but I was so hopelessly jealous of Nicholas I couldn't see it. I'm not proud of that. But I never made love to you for revenge as you thought. I wanted you so very much that first night and the next morning... I nearly went out of my mind when I saw those suits. The poison started to work again. That man was encroaching on my world. He was someone threatening my happiness and yet was an unknown quantity. A part of your life that I wasn't.

'When I came back to the apartment the following week I knew I had to be rid of him once and for all—his clothes, everything. You saw nothing wrong in his staying with you but I couldn't stand it. If you had stopped me I don't know what I would have done. Then later when I met him it hit me just what I had done to myself and you: tortured us both for nothing.'

'You said something to Nicholas after he'd nearly hit you and I'd left the pair of you.'

'Seeing him, I realised you couldn't possibly be romantically involved with him.' He grinned at her and smoothed a kiss across her chin. 'Not your sort, not man enough for you.'

'Oh, Mel,' Jade laughed, tightening her arms around his neck. 'You really are a pig. Nicholas is—'

'Nicholas was a hero,' he interrupted in a conciliatory tone. 'I must admit he stuck up for you when he thought I had wronged you. I admire him for that.'

'That's what friends are for.'

Mel kissed her again, more deeply this time. His hands moved to the front of her silk shirt. 'Well, that particular friend—'

'That particular friend is coming down on Sunday. With his fiancée,' Jade added quickly. She planted a kiss firmly on his mouth. 'Now if that isn't a test of your love, Mel, I can't think of—'

'Anything worse,' Mel groaned, and lowered his mouth to the warm, scented valley between her breasts. His kiss was seductive and sublime, and she read his unspoken message. Nicholas wasn't a threat any more, just a nuisance perhaps.

'We don't have long, then,' Mel told her, slipping the shirt from her shoulders. 'A day and a bit and a couple of nights and it isn't nearly enough, my darling.'

'After that . . .' she helped him with his sweater ' . . . we have a lifetime.'

'Mmm, but with all these weddings coming up . . .' He helped her with the zip of her skirt.

'Weddings?' she murmured dreamily. She fumbled with the belt of his corduroy jeans.

'This Nicholas of yours and hopefully Nadia and Dave's, and, of course, your father's.'

'My father's?' Jade uttered weakly as he grazed passionate kisses across her throat.

'Mmm, didn't I tell you? We exchanged confidences. I told him something I should have told him four years ago—that I had every intention of marrying his daughter—and that was why he was so happy to let me have Ritchie's. Then he told me about his lady, Anita, and how he's planning on—'

'I don't care what he's planning,' Jade muttered as her heart raced, and the fire inside her roared as he held her, naked at last, pressed tightly against him on the sofa, a real fire crackling in the background. 'Weddings, weddings,' she breathed.

'And most importantly ours, darling,' he murmured. 'Our union, like this, special and perfect and inevitable.'

She closed all around him, her body, her heart, her very soul wrapping him in love. This man who had given her so much trouble would soon be her special husband and their children would be special and their whole life would be so... so special.

'I love you so very much, my darling,' they whispered in unison, and then laughed, and suddenly everything was right with the world.

EPILOGUE

JADE stopped in the doorway of the drawing room and gazed at Mel propping up the bar. The spectre of him standing there four years ago—gosh, it was four and a half years now—had been well and truly exorcised. Though he was chatting quite happily to her father now, she knew he was uncomfortable. He had always loathed parties.

She went to him as her father moved away to join his beloved Anita and the other guests. She hooked her arm in his and gave him a loving squeeze.

'Can you bear it?' She grinned up at him.

Mel gazed down at her adoringly. 'Only because I know what's coming this time.' He lifted her chin and kissed the tip of her nose.

'You're going to have to get used to it. Daddy's a party animal and now he's back in the UK for good he'll find every excuse to throw one.'

Mel groaned and then grinned at her. 'I'll suffer anything for you.'

'You'd better,' she teased, then squeezed his hand tightly, and he lifted it and kissed the diamond ring on her engagement finger. 'With this ring...' he started to murmur.

'Shush.' Jade giggled softly. 'Daddy's about to make one of his famous speeches.'

'This one I can bear,' Mel whispered in her ear.

And John Ritchie stood up and made his announcement—several in fact. He congratulated Nicholas and Trisha on their engagement and said if they

186

didn't hurry up and get married it would be the longest engagement in history. He congratulated Nadia and Dave Rand on their whirlwind romance and engagement. Then he announced his own engagement to Anita and said how the woman he loved had threatened him with pain of death unless he made a decent woman of her. And then he announced the best bit of all—the engagement of his beautiful daughter to Mel Biaggio. And he was still extolling their virtues as Jade and Mel quietly slipped out of the French doors, immediately breaking into a run across the velvety green lawns of Bankton House.

Giggling and breathless, Jade fell into Mel's arms outside the summer house.

'Oh, you were so brave, darling,' she laughed as Mel nuzzled her hair.

'I told you I'd suffer anything for you.' His mouth closed firmly over hers and she clung to him, lost in his love and the depth of the kiss. He drew back from her at last and grinned down at her. 'I kind of liked it, actually. Perhaps I'll get used to it after a while. There are going to be a lot more announcements in the future, after all.'

'Oh, yes, what?' she asked laughingly, her eyes dancing with happiness.

'Wedding plans. Birth announcements. I think there might be a few of those as you have nothing better to do with your time...'

She sprang back from him with a squeal, wagging her finger at him. 'Now don't you give me any trouble, Mel Biaggio.'

'Don't tempt me,' he laughed, and gathered her up into his arms and carried her into the summer house, kicking the door shut with the back of his heel.

'Mel!' Jade cried, and then there was silence...

MILLS & BOON®

Next Month's Romances

♡

Each month you can choose from a wide variety of romance novels from Mills & Boon. Below are the new titles to look out for next month from the Presents and Enchanted series.

Presents™

Enchanted™

MILLS & BOON®

TO HAVE & TO HOLD

Celebrate the joy, excitement and sometimes
mishaps that occur when planning that special
wedding in our treasured four-story collection.

Written by four talented authors—
Barbara Bretton, Rita Clay Estrada,
Sandra James and Debbie Macomber

Don't miss this wonderful short story collection
for incurable romantics everywhere!

Available: April 1997   Price: £4.99

*Available from WH Smith, John Menzies, Volume One, Forbuoys, Martins, Woolworths,
Tesco, Asda, Safeway and other paperback stockists.*

MILLS & BOON®

By Request™

Bestselling romances brought
back to you by popular demand

◆

Two complete novels in one volume by bestselling author

Emma
Goldrick

The Unmarried Bride

The Widow's Mite

Available: April 1997   Price: £4.50

FOUR FREE
specially selected
Presents™ novels
PLUS a FREE Mystery Gift
when you return this page...

Return this coupon and we'll send you 4 Mills & Boon® Presents™ novels and a mystery gift absolutely FREE! We'll even pay the postage and packing for you.

We're making you this offer to introduce you to the benefits of the Reader Service™– FREE home delivery of brand-new Mills & Boon Presents novels, at least a month before they are available in the shops, FREE gifts and a monthly Newsletter packed with information, competitions, author profiles and lots more...

Accepting these FREE books and gift places you under no obligation to buy, you may cancel at any time, even after receiving just your free shipment. Simply complete the coupon below and send it to:

MILLS & BOON READER SERVICE, FREEPOST, CROYDON, SURREY, CR9 3WZ.

READERS IN EIRE PLEASE SEND COUPON TO PO BOX 4546, DUBLIN 24

NO STAMP NEEDED

Yes, please send me 4 free Presents novels and a mystery gift. I understand that unless you hear from me, I will receive 6 superb new titles every month for just £2.20* each, postage and packing free. I am under no obligation to purchase any books and I may cancel or suspend my subscription at any time, but the free books and gift will be mine to keep in any case. (I am over 18 years of age)

P7XE

Ms/Mrs/Miss/Mr _____

BLOCK CAPS PLEASE

Address_____

_____

_____ Postcode _____

SANDRA BROWN

New York Times bestselling author

HONOUR BOUND

Theirs was an impossible love

"One of fiction's brightest stars!"
—Dallas Morning News

Lucas Greywolf was Aislinn's forbidden fantasy—and every moment of their mad dash across Arizona drew her closer to this unyielding man.

MIRA®

AVAILABLE IN PAPERBACK
FROM MARCH 1997